A WINDOW OF SKY

In this sequel to *A Small Piece of Paradise* and *A Touch of Magic*, Joe is growing up. His friend Mr Massiter had had another attack and was seriously ill and Mrs Massiter needed him. As he turned into the drive of the large white house, he had little idea of the changes that would affect his life so deeply. Joe and his donkey Smokey go to live in the country with Mrs Massiter. Can he find a life where he feels he really belongs?

A WINDOW OF SKY

A WINDOW OF SKY

by
Geoffrey Morgan

Dales Large Print Books
Long Preston, North Yorkshire,
England.

British Library Cataloguing in Publication Data.

Morgan, Geoffrey
  A window of sky.

  A catalogue record for this book is
  available from the British Library

  ISBN 1-85389-635-7 pbk

First published in Great Britain by Collins, 1969

Published in Large Print July, 1996 by arrangement with
Geoffrey Morgan.

Dales Large Print is an imprint of
Library Magna Books Ltd.
Printed and bound in Great Britain by
T.J. Press (Padstow) Ltd., Cornwall, PL28 8RW.

For Ann
because of Tuesday

Chapter One

Joe reached London the day the news broke. All the way up from Shelbourne he had seen the flaring black headlines spelling out the death of the Company. He couldn't get away from the news. Papers were everywhere. All carried the front page story. Pictures, too.

It was a strange, unreal feeling seeing Arnold Massiter's likeness there, framed in the black type. It had a kind of sad finality. Like the picture of a captain whose ship has gone down...

Winthrop Property Developments, the Company that had put up some of the tallest buildings in London, suddenly appeared to have no foundations itself—that's how one City Editor put it...*Difficulties had been evident in recent months,* assessed another correspondent, *no doubt in part due to the absences of the Chairman, who has not been a well man...*

Joe hadn't realised that Mr Massiter had been ill again. Shut away all term at Shelbourne, of course, he hadn't been able to see for himself, though he should have read between the lines of Mrs Massiter's letters. She'd mentioned that he'd been working too hard; that the Company's affairs were causing a good deal of worry, but she hadn't hinted just how bad they really were. Still, he should have been prepared for—well, *something*, when she'd asked him to come home a week before the end of term; but it was still a shock when he'd seen the headlines that morning on the bookstall at Shelbourne station.

It had been a slow journey. Grey December fog shrouded the Hampshire countryside, and landmarks made familiar on the journeys at the beginning and end of term were vague, confused shapes almost beyond recognition. Joe's thoughts were rather like that. Vague. Confused. Even after reading the news report twice, the underlying reason for the crash was no clearer. What had gone wrong? There must

10

have been some warning. Why didn't Mrs Massiter tell him? But he knew the answer to that one. She wouldn't want to worry him—upset his studies. It was silly really. Putting it off. In the end you had to know. But then she was a woman and she loved him as his mother might have done. Of course, she *was* his mother in the legal sense. Adopted mother. Although within himself he still thought of her and her husband as Mr and Mrs Massiter, they were really the only parents he had known.

There was no fog at Waterloo. Just a faint, damp haze that misted the lights of the station and gave a coloured halo to the Christmas tree. There were a lot of people waiting; but no one waiting for him. Someone was always there when his train pulled in. Usually it was Mrs Massiter with Jenkins parked outside in the Rover; but if anything kept her away—and few events did—then the chauffeur would come on his own. But not this time. Not that he would have expected it now.

Early editions of the evening papers were

already on sale. But the headlines were different. Some other disaster had wiped the morning story away. An air crash somewhere. Joe had no idea where. He didn't want to know. The crash of the Company was enough for him. If there was further news inside he didn't want to read it. He'd hear the whole story when he got home.

He took a taxi to Eleigh Place. This was no time for extravagance; but there was no other way of getting there fast. The sky was low and darkening above Waterloo Bridge, pressing down as if to suffocate the brave glow of the fairyland lights festooning the Embankment. The streets were choked with traffic so the drive northward through WC2 to NW1 was slow, frustrating. No one seemed good tempered, even with Christmas so near. The decorated shop windows brought the season closer still, but somehow the spirit wasn't there. Or perhaps Joe couldn't feel it. Certainly, it didn't seem like Christmas; that was a time for hope. And Joe's hopes had been sinking all day.

It was quieter when they neared Regent's Park and turned into Eleigh Place. The wide, tree-lined road was empty and each exclusive residence lay back in sombre isolation brooding darkly behind its neat clusters of shrubs and trees. Here and there a lighted window glowed, but Joe got no warmth from it.

He felt no better when he paid off the taxi and walked between the white-pillared gateway of Number Seven. The branches of the bare trees edging the drive formed a filigree pattern against the lighted background of the raised porch. The impressive white front of the house with its tall windows and balcony was familiar enough now; yet this time he approached like a stranger. He had a sickly, apprehensive feeling inside. His feet seemed to drag on the damp gravel as he skirted the lawn and reached the steps of the porch. It reminded him of his first visit... A cheeky urchin in a grubby jersey with a weasel in a box and nothing to support him but his confidence. The boy had had a sickly feeling, too, and his knees were knocking; but he'd pressed the bell—and look what he'd become...

The place was very quiet. In the closeness of the porch Joe could feel the silence. A tense, ominous silence as if the house itself was awaiting some further disaster. His finger probed the stillness when he pressed the bell.

Parker opened the door. The same Parker who had once tried to run him off the premises. The man was smaller now, thinner, his back slightly bent. Time tolling away in the lines of his face. He had always appeared a rather sombre figure, and his dark-tailed suit and black tie seemed to emphasise the present occasion, though he would never think of appearing on duty in anything else.

'Good evening, Mr Joe.' Parker drew the door wide and leaned forward, taking Joe's bag. 'I'm so glad you've come, sir.'

Joe stepped inside and the butler closed the door.

'You've heard, of course?' The old man spoke in a hushed voice.

'It was in all the papers.' Joe could see

how the news had affected him. It was in the lost look of the eyes, the weakness of the smile when he'd greeted Joe, the droop of the shoulders.

'Yes, the papers, to be sure.' He shook his head. 'Tragic,' he murmured. 'Tragic.' He reached to take Joe's coat, but Joe peeled it off and threw it with his school cap over the dark oak settle, and stepped out of the front lobby into the great semi-circular hall.

The lights were low. The crystal chandelier below the high ceiling was unlit. Everything was bathed in the soft glow of the four standard lamps edging the wall with another at the head of the wide staircase lighting the gallery above. There were no decorations, only some tall ferns and winter Jasmine in the alabaster urns and a bowl of Christmas roses on one of the side tables. The library door was ajar, but the room was in darkness. The lounge door was open, too. One of the table lamps was on and he could see the glow of the fire's reflection on the further wall. No one was there.

Joe paused in the centre, looking round. 'Where is everyone, Parker?' he asked.

The old man hesitated, glancing at the plain gold clock on the pedestal beside the stairs.

'Madam should have returned by now,' he said.

'Returned from where?'

'The nursing home.'

Joe stared. He didn't say anything. He waited for Parker to tell him. But he knew.

'It's the Master,' Parker said. 'Yesterday he was ill again. But he wouldn't give in. He had to carry on. The Company's affairs, you see. People came. Hordes of people, coming and going all day.'

Joe could see them. Lawyers, liquidators, Company representatives. Thinking of the money, not of the man.

'Madam advised him to rest. Sir Vincent insisted he saw no one. It made no difference. He thought he was capable of carrying on, here, in his home.'

'And now—' Joe faltered. 'He's very ill?'

'In the night he was. Things were a little better this morning. But Sir Vincent would take no more chances, and when he came again this afternoon the ambulance followed him. Madam went with him.'

'What time was that?'

Parker glanced at the clock again, and at that moment its soft chimes flowed six times through the silence of the hall. He looked back at Joe.

'It must have been a few minutes after three,' he reflected.

'And she's not back yet. I'd better go.'

'She must be on her way now,' Parker said. 'In fact, I thought it was madam when you rang the bell. She telephoned a short while ago and said he was a little better. That she would be leaving soon. She wanted to know if you'd arrived, and as soon as you did I was to serve you some food.'

'I'm not hungry,' Joe said. 'If she doesn't come soon I'll go to the nursing home.'

'Of course, Mr Joe,' he nodded gravely. 'But give madam a little more time. Can I get you something? A drink perhaps? Some coffee?'

'I could drink something,' Joe said. 'Coffee would be nice. Give me the bag, Parker. I'll go and clean up while you attend to it.'

Joe hurried upstairs. He had grown fond of Parker. Parker was one of the old-fashioned kind. If he appeared a little pompous, slightly superior to the uninvited, it was only to emphasise the importance of his calling as the principal servant of the household; a responsibility that required all his tact and understanding, not only in dealing with his own staff, but in defending his master's privacy from the outside world. Underneath he was warm, friendly, wise and sympathetic, as Joe had learned since that first meeting; as was evident now.

Two of the pictures were missing from the gallery that formed the wide landing at the top of the stairs which followed the curve of the hall for half its length. Joe thought they were the Goya and the Degas; but he wasn't sure. He wasn't very interested in paintings, unless they were landscapes, like the Constable at the end.

But the best picture of all was in his

18

bedroom. And it wasn't a painting. It was a large coloured photograph of a donkey. It was taken at Valley End. Smokey was standing at his stable door looking straight at the camera with his ears cocked, his eyes large and doleful and wisps of hay protruding either side of his muzzle like cat's whiskers.

The picture hung on the wall opposite the bed and was like a window of country with Smokey looking through it right on to Joe's pillow. Sometimes in the faint rays of the lamp outside it seemed like it really was a window; as if the picture came to life, and Joe was sure Smokey had flicked his ears or moved his jaws or blinked his eyes. But, of course, it had only been a trick of the light, and wishful thinking on Joe's part. Still, it was a nice thought to go to bed with, and it served to remind him that whatever the obstacles, some day, somehow, he would go back to the freedom of the country, and have a donkey like Smokey again.

Joe washed and changed his shirt, and was on his way back along the landing when the front door bell rang. He paused at the head of the stairs, looking down into the hall as he heard Parker open the door. He stood there, waiting to see the caller and knowing the caller was Mrs Massiter.

She came into the light of the hall first, followed by a slim, elderly man with white hair. Even in the soft lights he recognised the elegant, darkly dressed figure of Sir Vincent Craig. Joe wondered why he had returned, then realised he had brought Mrs Massiter back in his car as she had gone in the ambulance.

He went down the stairs and she didn't see him at first. She turned to speak to Parker, who answered with a glance across the hall. Joe stepped from the carpeted treads to the parquet floor as she swung round.

'Hullo, Mother,' he said. He could see her clearly now. Her mouth showed deep red in the paleness of her face. Her eyes, always warm and brown, looked black, lifeless, in the shadows surrounding them.

'Joe!' she said. 'Oh—Joe.' Her voice was

tight, controlled. He could feel the pressure of her fingers on his shoulders, and her wet cheeks against his face. She stood there, holding on to him, trembling a little but saying nothing.

And Joe knew that Arnold Massiter was dead.

Chapter Two

It had all begun with Mr Penny. His donkey had something to do with it, too. Smokey pulled the junkman's little cart through the East End streets, and it was there that Joe had met them. After that there was never a spare moment when you wouldn't find Joe at the junk-yard in Sparrow Street. Not so much in the yard, mind you, as in the house at the end of it or the garden at the back of it. For Mr Penny and Joe seemed to have the same interests (outside the junk trade, that is)—a fondness for animals, and a love of the country, and this had manifested itself in the garden they had created behind the yard.

Joe was quite small then, but big enough to appreciate the friendship and kindness of a man like Mr Penny, while the old man found Joe a cheery young companion whose warmth and wonder took away some of the loneliness in his life.

Joe lived quite close to Sparrow Street. In Palfrey Buildings. He lived with Aunt Ethel and his sister Liz, and sometimes Uncle Bert who went to sea on a cargo ship. Joe never went anywhere, except to school, of course, so it was nice to pop round to Sparrow Street whenever he was free, knowing there was a welcome there. For the garden behind the yard was not only a lush oasis in a drab world of brick and mortar, it was a natural sanctuary for all Joe's pets which he could never have kept in Aunt Ethel's flat. So meeting Mr Penny couldn't have been a happier arrangement really, but happiness only lasts so long, as Joe discovered when Arnold Massiter came.

It was the Council that was to blame; they were making development plans for sites in Greenham Borough. Mr Penny's property just happened to be one of them. Mr Massiter's company had bought the site next door, and wanted Mr Penny to sell. The old man had lived there a very long time and wouldn't give up his home without a fight, but he wasn't much of a fighter. It was Joe who'd gone to see Mr Massiter in his house in Regent's Park. He wasn't sure what he could do when he got there, but he'd taken Tinker, his pet weasel, in support of the cause. Finding the house in Eleigh Place had been comparatively easy; finding the owner was very difficult. Mr Massiter was out, and the butler wouldn't allow Joe to wait, and in the scrimmage that followed Tinker escaped into the garden. And that was how Joe met Mrs Massiter.

Laura Massiter was a lonely woman. She was a little on the plain side, too, but that had nothing to do with her loneliness. No woman should be lonely when she's married, but *she* was—the result of being married to a fast-moving property tycoon like Arnold Massiter. If her looks were not particularly noticeable, her voice was a charmer, and her warm, generous character more than compensated for any shortcomings in the way of physical beauty. She was an understanding person, faithful to the things she held dear; sensible, with a fair sense of justice as well as a sense of humour. But she was also a woman. She needed affection, companionship and children. Everything else was there; all the material things, but the three things she wanted most were missing. She had lost a child the year after marriage, and somehow in the race to the top, all the tender, personal things got left behind. So there was tension and breaking strains when she met Joe.

The little boy from the East End with his confident request to see her husband was an unexpected diversion for her, and she warmed to him at once. They found Tinker, and Joe stayed to tea, telling her the story he'd brought for her husband. And afterwards she drove him back to Sparrow Street to see the garden and the pets and to meet Mr Penny and his donkey.

She had been sympathetic from the first, and promised to do what she could, but her vain efforts to save Mr Penny's home and garden only finalised the rift in her marriage. She moved out of Eleigh Place and went down to Valley End, her small house in Suffolk, and it was there she invited Joe and Mr Penny when the end came. But the end was very different from what they expected. It was tragedy. For the tower crane on the adjoining building site had crashed down in a storm and crumpled Mr Penny's house. And the old man was dead when they found him.

That had been the first real turning point in Joe's life. Losing Mr Penny. For he had gone back to Valley End with Mrs Massiter, where Smokey and all Joe's pets were awaiting him. It was a logical solution to the tragedy, and it opened the way for Laura Massiter to set in motion the hopes she had harboured in her own mind over the past months. The legal adoption of Joe. All the other circumstances seemed to fall into place to support her, for with Aunt Ethel recuperating with her baby in Brighton and Liz on the way to becoming engaged and Uncle Bert nursing a broken leg in Australia, there was no doubt where Joe should be. And he was already there.

Those first weeks at Valley End did Joe no end of good. They brought the colour back into his freckled face and softened the numbing blow of the tragic events in Sparrow Street. His sorrow began to fade in the excitement of discovering a world that lay open to the sky. At last he was where he had always wanted to be—right in the heart of the country. There were new things to learn, new people to meet, new sights to see; so many new experiences, and all to be shared with Smokey.

Joe went to school, of course, for his education, but he reckoned he learned much more from Ben Pollard. About the real things, that is. Like the scents and rhythm of country life, the effect of the season on plant and animal, the rotation of the crops, and the habits of the wild creatures who lived in Marley Wood. Ben knew about these things. He lived close to the earth and the earth revealed its secrets. He didn't seem to worry about money; he scratched a living from his garden produce and a few hens that surrounded his old cottage. He didn't make many friendships, but he welcomed Joe, and with his knowledge and rustic independence, he became a kind of hero to the boy, gradually taking the place in his life that Mr Penny had vacated.

They were happy days for Joe, secure in the knowledge that Mrs Massiter was happy, too. Her happiness was in giving; all she asked for in return was a little affection, a little companionship, a little knowledge that she was wanted again. And Joe gave her these things.

It was towards early summer, when the country sky was clear, that a dark thread of cloud appeared on Joe's horizon. That was the time the news came of Arnold Massiter's illness, and Mrs Massiter went to London to be with him. It was the time, too, that Uncle Bert arrived unexpectedly, on his way to join his ship, to tell Joe of the family's plan to emigrate to Australia. Joe didn't mind the family going so long as he could stay; that didn't worry him. But Mr Massiter did. Not just on account of his illness, but because of the effect this might have on life at Valley End. Joe didn't want the routine to change. Nor Mrs Massiter. Yet he wondered... Things did change people. Even someone as rigid as Mr Massiter. He'd never been quite the same since the accident in Sparrow Street. No doubt the countrywide publicity had something to do with that. He had certainly been sympathetic at the time. It seemed to make him aware that people should be considered as well as money and business. He began to make more time for the personal things. He'd called at Valley End on occasion. Had given Joe presents. Sent flowers to Mrs Massiter at Christmas. Things like that from a hard-headed business man who had never spared a moment from his business affairs, certainly made him different, though Joe had always been sure that nothing would ever really change him. But illness—well, that would give him more time to think. Time to change altogether. And this was the fear Joe harboured when Mr Massiter came to stay at Valley End.

Sir Vincent Craig had advised it. A nice long rest, he'd said. Somewhere quiet, in the country. So Mrs Massiter had made the offer. She had told Joe her husband's presence there would make no difference; would not affect the life of the household. But it did. Everything began to revolve around him. And as the weeks went by and his health returned you could see the relationship between them grow closer. He took more interest in Joe, too. He talked about Joe's education and his future, when they went for walks together. He thought Joe would make his mark in the business world; the property world. But that wasn't the world that interested Joe. He had his own ideas about the future, and they were concerned with living close to the earth, like Ben, not building on it. He didn't want to go away to school. He was sure Mrs Massiter wouldn't want him to go. But how much influence would she have in the matter if they made up their marriage again?

That was the pattern of things, and Joe knew how it was long before she told him that they had decided to give their marriage a second chance. He was happy for her, it was what she wanted; but inside he was sad because he knew that things could never be the same any more.

It was about this time that Mr Massiter flew off on a business trip abroad, and in his absence Joe tried to convince himself that things might not be so bad. There was nothing he could do about it, anyway, even if he wanted to, and with the Elmbridge flower show and fair coming up, he was forced to concentrate on the present and leave the future to come. For he'd entered Smokey for the donkey race, and if he followed Ben's advice on training it was going to take all his attention and time.

It was in September, the day before the show, that Joe met Nina. The marquees were up in the meadow and the fair had assembled, and Saturday promised to be an exciting day. Joe sat outside Smokey's stable in the afternoon sun polishing the harness, and that was when he first saw the girl.

Nina was raven-haired and blue-eyed and helped her parents with their chimpanzee act, though she herself had ambitions

31

for the ballet. They were on their way to the fair in a Land-Rover and two caravans, but the radiator had boiled dry and she came seeking a can of water. She fell in love with Smokey and was so long appearing with the water that her mother began to call. They hurried down to the road then, Joe taking the can, and he was introduced to Leo and Lavina Steed and met the chimpanzees. They were a cheerful family and offered him a free seat at their show, and he promised to be there on Saturday. But when Saturday came it wasn't the day he'd expected.

In fact, it was the most confused and unsettled weekend Joe could remember. What with Mrs Massiter not feeling well, and Smokey getting lost for hours, and Mr Massiter arriving, it wasn't till Monday evening, after the Massiters had driven off to London, that he got to the fair.

But it was worth waiting for. Just to see it took your breath away. The fair had everything. It was big, gaudy, coloured, loud with people and music; a bursting bubble of light in the darkness of the meadow. They went through every sideshow, Joe and Nina; rode on every screeching amusement. It was a lovely evening. The only thing that spoiled it was the news when he got back to Valley End. The housekeeper was discussing it with her husband, and Joe overheard as he let himself in.

He still couldn't believe it when he got to bed. It kept him awake most of the night. It didn't seem possible Mrs Massiter was going to have a baby. That was why they'd gone to London—to see a specialist... The scraps of conversation between the housekeeper and her husband went round and round in his head... *They'll move to London now, to be sure... What about the boy then, and the donkey?... The boy will go to college, I s'ppose—Gawd knows what they'll do with the donkey...*

Joe had made up his mind by the morning. He didn't feel wanted now. And he wouldn't go away to college. He didn't want to leave the valley. He'd never leave Smokey. So he knew what he must do. He would go to Ben. He'd work for him.

There was sure to be some job he could find. Anything, if Ben would take them in. Ben would understand. You could rely on him.

But when he reached the cottage Ben wasn't there. The village policeman was in the house. He told Joe the story. Ben had been arrested for stealing game from Darren Hall. Joe saw the tools of the poacher's trade Ben had kept hidden in the cottage, and he tried to turn away from the truth. But he had to accept it... A poacher and a thief. That's what Ben was. He didn't really care for the wild creatures Joe held dear; he simply turned them into money. All the affection and admiration Joe had for Ben slowly drained away. And there was no one to turn to now. Nowhere to go. Smokey was his only friend.

Daylight was fading when he returned to Valley End. He went to the paddock for Smokey. He hugged the donkey to him and gazed across the valley. The fair was coming to life. The lights were twinkling and the music began to play. And suddenly he knew. There was still one place to go after all...

He left a note for Mrs Massiter, packed his canvas duffel bag, and set off with Smokey to the fair. He hadn't any doubts now. His hopes were high again. There'd be a job he could do; a place for him and Smokey. He'd go straight to the Steeds. Nina had told him her father was always needing help. He was sure there'd be a welcome there.

It was dark when boy and donkey left the lane and entered the gateway beyond the village road, but the fair was an island glow across the meadow. The jostling, noisy crowd, the leaping shadows and the hurdy-gurdy bump and grind of the organ music filled Joe with a tense anticipation. He hurried Smokey along the track beside the hedge dividing Spring Meadows, and he didn't hear the motor cycles on the other side. Four, there were. Youths from Lotchford, trick-riding amongst themselves, dangerously cutting across each other, forcing the pace until one gave way. And one gave way. Came through the gap in the hedge just as Joe and Smokey reached it.

Joe felt the donkey shudder. The thud and screech of metal swamped his senses. He knew he was falling... The lights of the roundabout spun faster and faster, and then there was nothing but the blackness of the sky.

When he opened his eyes there were shadows around him. And gradually the shadows became people. There were lights. Voices. He didn't feel any pain, but he couldn't seem to move. And all he could think of was Smokey. He thought he called the donkey's name. Someone must have heard. Someone kneeling close to him, bending over him. Such a small white face and dark hair, reminding him of Nina. It *was* Nina. He could see her eyes now. Moist and glistening, as if there were tears in them. And her lips were moving...

'It's all right, Joe,' she said. 'I'll take care of Smokey.'

But Joe didn't seem to be there at all...

The accident in Spring Meadows was another turning point in life. Because when Joe left the hospital he went back to London with the Massiters with no wish to go to Valley End again. There was nothing there except memories. It had been part of growing up. And growing up is happiness and excitement, disappointment and disillusion. It's sadness, too. For the saddest part of all was losing Smokey. His injuries had been much worse than the broken ribs and concussion that Joe had suffered, and they had to put him to sleep. So in a way Joe welcomed Shelbourne. To begin with. It was something entirely different and took his mind off the past.

It was a public school in the old tradition, housed in low-gabled, rambling buildings with ivy on the walls. It stood in broad playing fields in a wide Hampshire valley. The village was not far away, and the school boundary was a stream where the trout played in the shadow of willow trees. So Joe was in the country just the same. But it wasn't the same. The routine, the discipline, the sports field and the study, allowed little time for the great outside. So although he saw the country, and occasionally the animals in it, it was detached; his was a world in itself. Enclosed. Frustrating, it was. Not doing what he really wanted. But how many people could?

Nina could. She'd managed it. She was in Vienna. Working hard at the ballet. He hadn't seen her for a long time, but they corresponded. He didn't write at length; he hadn't the heart to enthuse about the things he did, perhaps because inside he didn't really want to do them. But Nina wrote long letters filled with her exciting progress.

So did Aunt Ethel. She always sent a letter on his birthday and at Christmas. From Australia. The family had settled down there. And it was lovely. Aunt Ethel was always telling him how lovely life was out there, and how lucky he was to be getting a proper education. He was glad they were happy. That they'd got what they wanted in the end. Liz, too. A baby already, and on the way to Australia herself, Ron being in the building trade, and Australia wanting builders.

It was nice to know they were happy. Some people were. He should have been, too. And in a way he was. Happy to know that he was making the Massiters happy doing what *they* wanted. He owed them something. Everything. It was one way to repay. And how could he ever make up for the loss he had caused Mrs Massiter? The baby she had hoped for had died within her almost before it had lived. She'd never told him so, but he knew the miscarriage she'd suffered was the result of the shock he had caused the night he'd run away to the fair.

He had a long way to go to make up for that. But he was trying, trying to be a dutiful son, although he knew it was sufficient for her to know that he was now a permanent member of the family. His affection for her was enough. She was satisfied.

Mr Massiter was satisfied, too. Perhaps for a different family reason. He saw Joe as a son who would follow him into the Company. Someone to take over the reins when the time came. Joe appreciated this.

Understood. To study hard and go into the Company was the least he could do for everything he'd been given, including such expensive education. Some day, perhaps, he might go back to the simpler things, the natural things, the lasting values that were synonymous with country life. But meanwhile, his course must be set by Mr Massiter's plans.

So he had studied hard, passed through the school and after next summer he'd take his place at university. And then there would be the Company. That was Mr Massiter's plan.

But now... Now there was no Company. And even Mr Massiter had gone...

Chapter Three

Sir Vincent Craig only stayed a few minutes. He left some sedatives for Mrs Massiter and told her to ring if she needed him. Joe went with him to the door and they shook hands, and Joe thanked him for all he had done.

'Take care of her, my boy,' Sir Vincent said in his quiet, suave voice. 'It's been a great strain these past months and now—the final shock. She's a resilient woman, but it takes time to bounce back from these things.' He paused on the steps of the porch and added, 'Take her away for Christmas. Somewhere with a little life, but not too boisterous. Do you both good.'

'Yes, sir,' Joe said. 'I'll do that.'

She was in the lounge when Joe went back. Staring into the fire. She looked up as he entered.

'Parker's bringing some coffee,' she said

softly. 'But I think I'd like a drink right now.'

Joe nodded and went to the cabinet in the corner.

'What will it be, Mother?'

'Oh, brandy, please, dear. Make it a strong one.'

He sorted the bottles around and paused with a glass in his hand.

'Not too much if you're—er—taking tablets,' he said.

A suggestion of a smile briefly lightened her pale face and was gone.

'I shall be all right, Joe,' she said. 'I'm not falling back on drugs. The brandy will do more good.'

Parker came in a moment later with the coffee and some sandwiches. He served Mrs Massiter's black.

'Cook insisted on the sandwiches, ma'am,' he explained almost apologetically. 'Chicken here—and these, fresh salmon and cucumber.' He put the shallow silver dishes on the low table.'

She nodded her thanks. 'Joe will eat them.

Parker went out, closing the door noiselessly, and Joe remained standing, idly stirring his coffee, looking down at her.

'You've been travelling most of the day, Joe,' she said. 'You must be hungry.'

'Not really. And I don't suppose you've eaten at all yourself.' He offered her the dish, but she shook her head. A dark curl with a hint of silver in it fell across her forehead. When she pushed it back he could see the deep lines above her brow.

'Sit down, dear,' she said. 'And talk to me. What sort of journey did you have?'

'Oh, you know, the usual. Foggy. Slow.' But it wasn't the usual at all. There was too much in the papers for that. Not that he would mention it, however much he wished to know the whole story. She would tell him when she was ready and he would wait till then.

He sat down in the armchair opposite, sipping his coffee because he didn't know what to say. The hearth-rug looked empty between them and he suddenly imagined a cat sitting there. What a difference a cat would make. Or a dog. Either sprawled between them on the rug would have brought a certain aura of comfort, created a distraction. Animals needed your attention and affection whatever the circumstances; they would have been a reason to talk when you weren't sure what to say.

She was looking at him over her glass, frowning a little.

'Aren't you going to eat something?' she asked.

He put down his cup and took a sandwich.

'You know,' she went on, 'I really think you've got thinner. I thought so when you were standing just now. What have you been doing at school?'

'The same old things, but a bit more exercise. The new gym, and some cross-country running. But I haven't lost any weight.' He glanced down at himself. 'I think it's this suit—it's sort of waisted.'

He didn't want to talk about himself. Or the past. He supposed it was the shock that helped to avoid the present. Certainly she wouldn't want to talk about that. Not now. It might help to look ahead a bit. The future was better to think about. Going away for Christmas, for instance. That's what Sir Vincent had said. Going away from this great house, which now seemed strangely empty.

He re-filled her coffee cup and sat down, leaning forward.

'I don't know whether Sir Vincent mentioned it to you,' he said. 'But he gave me some advice.'

She looked at him wonderingly.

'He's always been a good friend,' she said. 'What did he say to you?'

'He suggested that we should go away —you know, after—everything—for Christmas. He said it would do you good.'

'Perhaps it would. I don't know.' Her gaze fell slowly to her glass, and there was a distant look in her eyes. Her voice seemed far away, too. 'I haven't thought about it—I haven't thought about anything.'

'Of course not,' Joe said. 'But I think he's right. And if you'd like me to think about it, you have only to nod your head.'

The faint smile momentarily touched her lips again.

'All right, Joe,' she said slowly. 'You think about it, and we'll see.'

Joe really had no need to think about it. He knew Sir Vincent's advice was sensible. And he was ready to admit that he was selfish enough to want to get away himself. In the days that followed he could see that Mrs Massiter would welcome an opportunity to go, too.

There seemed so many duties to perform, and there was a hushed kind of urgency permeating the house. There were the callers and the flowers and the letters and all the arrangements to be made. Joe wanted to help and he was able to in minor ways, but mostly Mrs Massiter wanted to do it all herself. It had to be done, and it kept her mind active, and it was better that way. But when it was over and the reaction set in, Joe was sure that going away from the place if only for Christmas would counteract it.

Although time was so short for booking he had several travel agents searching for a suitable hotel, and on the morning of the funeral an agent in Baker Street rang to say they thought they could offer the perfect place. Joe arranged to go in next day, but he kept the news to himself.

They buried Mr Massiter at Stavinton in the little churchyard overlooking the Downs. That was his wish. That's where his family were. It was a lovely day for December. The morning mist had gone and the southerly wind brought a tang of sea with it over the Downs, rustling the yews and elms sheltering the church. There were broad corridors of sky etched deeply blue between cloud patches that gleamed foamy white in the sun. Across the slopes and lowlands the many-coloured pattern of the fields were an ever-changing scene of sunlight and shadow, with here and there the darker hues of grazing sheep and cattle. The country looked so bright and clean and alive that it made you even more sad to think of someone who'd never see it again.

It was a simple ceremony. But impressive. Not many people. Mostly strangers to

Joe. Even the few relations. They came over to speak to Mrs Massiter when everything was over, but no one seemed able to say very much. Joe just stood there, watching the people leave in their cars.

Mr Stringer went by, the solicitor from Chancery Lane. He was one of the partners who had always looked after Mrs Massiter's legal affairs. Mr Stringer somehow looked like a solicitor, but Mr Dawson gave the opposite impression. He didn't look like a solicitor at all; but Mr Massiter had been his principal client. He was a shiny, jovial man, large and round with a double chin and a monocle; but his expression was solemn in conversation with Mr Rayner, a director of the Company.

When Joe saw Sir Vincent Craig standing alone near his car, he excused himself from the group and went across, but before he could say anything the vicar joined them. So Joe took the opportunity to thank him for the service, and Sir Vincent commented on the beauty of the church, which led the vicar to speak of its sad condition. It was in need of some repair. And always in need of money. The tower was in some danger and they couldn't ring the bells. But Mr Massiter had given generously in recent years and had sent down an architect, so the restoration would shortly begin. Things were moving. They owed a lot to Mr Massiter. He was a good man.

Joe had no idea Mr Massiter had given generously to the church, or to anything else. How could he know, being away at school most of the time? But remembering how the man had changed over the years there were probably a lot of good things about him that Joe didn't know.

They went back on their own in the hired car. Just Mrs Massiter and himself. All the others had gone before they left the village. On the way home the chauffeur had a bit of trouble with the oil warning light, and while he was having it checked they went into a sleepy cafe near the garage for a cup of tea. That seemed to revive Mrs Massiter; she hadn't said much so far. But when they resumed the journey she spoke about Sir Vincent's advice.

'I've been thinking about it, Joe,' she

said quietly. 'It seems to be the sensible thing. To get right away from everything, just for Christmas. The change will make such a difference, and perhaps give me a chance to think about our future.' She glanced at him. 'That is, if it's not too late to find anywhere. Did you do anything about it?'

He told her then about the travel agent in Baker Street.

'I'll go and see him in the morning,' he said.

In the morning, soon after ten, Joe was at the agent's office leafing through the brochure of the Pinewood Hotel. It was on the cliffs near Bournemouth. Rather select, the agent said. Not too big or noisy, but not dull either. Log fires and central heating and good Christmas fare. Very pleasant walks to Sandbanks and Poole Harbour, yet quite close to the centre of the town. The agent knew. He'd stayed there in October. On his honeymoon. Of course, he didn't know the particular two rooms available. They were singles. But he was certain of their comfort, and it was the only Christmas vacancy on his books. A cancellation, you see.

Joe got him to ring through immediately and waited for confirmation. It wasn't until he was out in the street that he remembered the tickets. The agent might as well get them, too, and there would be no delay at the station in the crowds on Christmas Eve.

He hurried back to the office. It was a pity really, they had to go by train, especially as he'd passed his driving test during the summer holidays, and would have liked to have got some more practice in. He knew there was little chance of that for the moment, for the Rover was in the Company's garage along with the Rolls, pending the liquidation. Everything, it seemed, was tied in with the Company.

Mr Stringer was there when Joe got back to the house. He came out of the library with a slim briefcase, talking earnestly to Mrs Massiter as they crossed the hall. Parker was in the lobby with the solicitor's hat and coat, ready to show him out. Joe slipped into the lounge and stood on the rug with his back to the fire, reading the hotel brochure. He went to the door when he knew Stringer had gone, and called to her across the hall.

'I've something to show you,' he said, waving the brochure. 'Come in and see.'

He could tell by her expression that she was distracted, concerned with something else.

'I've fixed it,' he went on. 'Bournemouth. Here, take a look, this is the hotel.' He put the brochure into her hand so she could see the illustrated cover. 'We're lucky. They had a cancellation.'

She glanced down at the picture without much interest.

'Very nice, Joe,' she said vaguely. 'But I don't know if we should go now. There's not much time.'

'Time?' He was puzzled. 'We've two days yet. I've booked from Christmas Eve. There's not much to pack.'

'I know—I wasn't meaning that. There's little time now for all we have to do. Only three months, in fact. I'm not sure we can

52

afford to lose even a few days by going away.'

Joe was surprised. He didn't understand.

'What d'you mean, Mother? Lose a few days? Only three months—for what?'

She looked at him anxiously.

'To get out of this house,' she said.

Chapter Four

It was like Sparrow Street all over again. Only this was Eleigh Place. And it didn't seem possible. Not Mr Massiter's house. But it wasn't his house any more. Hadn't been for some time. And now they had to go.

In Sparrow Street it had been the Council and the Company that had taken over; now the Company had gone and the creditors were waiting to take over what assets remained. That's how it looked to Joe. It was a sort of ironic justice really. Strange, how life had moved full circle in so brief a span of time.

He couldn't help remembering. It was the kind of shock that brought back the past. But although it was natural to make comparisons he had no right to compare the events; circumstances were so different. For now it was Mrs Massiter—he wasn't thinking of himself—who had to shoulder the burden.

Joe didn't ask any questions. She probably didn't know the answers yet. He could see she was only just beginning to find things out for herself. It certainly wasn't the moment to argue about going away. So it was just as well that the telephone rang, and Parker called to her from the hall.

Obviously Stringer had told her the news that morning. It was another shock to take. But it would lose its sting and she would accept it in the resilient way she had accepted everything else. He would come back to the subject of Bournemouth then. After all, three months was quite a way ahead. What would be lost in three days? And, anyway, what could you do over Christmas?

His spirits began to lighten, and as if to heighten them further he noticed her expression when she looked in at the door.

'That was Wendy on the 'phone,' she explained.

'Wendy?'

'You remember, Joe—Mrs Wainwright. She's an old friend of mine.'

Joe pondered and then remembered.

'She's the plump rather attractive lady with the auburn hair who talks very fast? I think I met her a couple of times last summer.'

Mrs Massiter smiled faintly and said, 'She's in town and I've invited her to lunch. You don't mind?'

'Of course not. It'll do us good. She seems a cheerful type.'

The thought of her visit had certainly cheered Mrs Massiter, and she went off to the kitchen to discuss lunch with the cook.

Wendy Wainwright arrived with the second post at noon. She didn't bring it, of course; it just happened that she coincided with the postman at the front door. Parker let her in and then went back for the mail, and Joe led the visitor to the lounge. Mrs Wainwright hadn't changed; she spoke rapidly, bouncing off one subject and into another in mid-sentence; but she

56

slowed down a little when she greeted Mrs Massiter. Joe poured them a drink and left them to themselves, and found Parker awaiting him in the hall.

'A letter for you, Mr Joe,' he said, handing over the long slim envelope. 'I've put the others on the desk in the library.'

Joe nodded and went into the library and closed the door. It was quiet in there and the letter was intriguing; he needed the silence to think. It was from Brookham Garage in Luxton Street, just off Berkeley Square, and the message was brief and polite.

Your esteemed order, he read, *is now to hand, and we await your further instructions.*

It was signed by the Sales Manager.

Joe knew there was some mistake even though it was addressed to him. He'd never even heard of Brookham Garage let alone given them an order. It was obviously something that Mr Massiter had ordered and, having read the papers, they were writing to Joe. But—how did they know about *him?*

He couldn't answer that, and it puzzled

him all through lunch. He was glad Mrs Wainwright was there. He didn't have to concentrate on conversation or think of what to say; he didn't get a chance to talk; and it was easier to get away smartly without explanations. He didn't want to tell Mrs Massiter about the letter until he knew what it was about. So he was grateful to Mrs Wainwright at that moment. He left them in the lounge still talking over coffee, and hurried to Berkeley Square.

Luxton Street was a narrow one leading off the Square, and he found Brookham Garage near the end of it. It consisted of a large showroom window in which were two expensive cars, and a narrow entry at the side. Just wide enough to take a car, the entry ran through an archway below the first storey of the building to a service yard at the rear.

Inside, between the new cars was a long leather sofa and a low table spread with motoring magazines and catalogues, and on the walls coloured pictures of famous racing cars. Right at the back were two glass-fronted offices, large and small. The small one with *Sales Manager* printed on the door was screened with frosted glass.

A girl came out of the larger office and asked if she could help and Joe introduced himself and told her about the letter. She was very polite and invited him to sit down while she went to announce him. He was too intrigued to sit down, and he stood watching the shape of her head and shoulders through the opaque glass of the manager's office. After a moment another figure took shape behind the glass, and then a dark-suited man with the sleeky appearance of the cars in the showroom, came out.

'Good afternoon, sir,' he said. 'I'm glad you've called. We were very sorry to hear about your father.'

Joe nodded, but didn't say anything.

'We weren't quite sure what to do,' went on the manager. 'Our instructions were to deliver on Christmas Eve, but in view of the unhappy circumstances we thought it advisable to get in touch with you.'

'I'm pleased you did,' Joe said. 'Because I don't know anything about it.'

'This is what we anticipated. It was to be a surprise, you see?' He smiled. 'Would you come this way, sir?'

Joe followed him, his mind now quite confused, through the door at the back of the showroom. They went down a corridor with offices on one side and an equipment store on the other, and came out in a large service bay that opened on to the yard. There were several cars there, but the manager suddenly came to a halt beside a small, gleaming white convertible. He tapped the dark hood with his fingers.

'This is the surprise,' he said. 'And she's all ready to go.'

Joe still couldn't understand the man. What was he leading up to? It was either some kind of joke or a glaring mistake.

'I don't understand,' he said.

The manager nodded, slipping into a more business-like manner. 'What happened is this. The late Mr Arnold M—er—your father asked us several weeks ago to order this car and to hold it till Christmas. He told us he wanted to give his son a surprise present, and we were instructed to have everything ready, and the car registered in your name and delivered to you at the house on Christmas Eve—tomorrow, in fact. But in the circumstances you will appreciate our decision to get in touch with—'

'You mean—this car is—mine?' Joe interrupted, staring at the gleaming model in a new light.

'Absolutely,' said the manager. 'Your father settled the account when he gave us the order.' He opened the driving door. 'Get in and see what she feels like.'

Joe got in. The smell of the new upholstery wrapped itself around him as he sank back in the seat. The walnut trim, the wood-rimmed steering wheel, and the stubby gear-shift on the floor filled him with exciting anticipation. There was a glove-box in the dash and a large rev counter and a host of other instruments; and the overall carpet was so thick it might have been in the lounge at home.

'How is she for size?' The manager was leaning close to the open window. 'You can see there's room for two in the back.'

Joe could see all right.

'Fantastic!' was all he could say. He was so thrilled and surprised and happy that some of his enthusiasm rubbed off on the manager even though the car was way below the expensive range of model he usually sold and the profit a great deal less.

'Of course, she's a standard model,' he went on, as if it was an exception to his normal business. 'But we've souped her up a little. Your father wanted everything complete down to the last detail. So we've fitted radial tyres, and supplied a tonneau cover and a spring steering wheel. And, of course, we thought you'd like the usual accessories—fog lamps, wing mirrors, radio—as you've probably noticed. The tank's full, and she's licenced and insured. Comprehensive, of course.'

Joe got out slowly, walking all round the car.

'And it's really mine?' he murmured. 'And there's—nothing—to pay?'

'Not a penny,' smiled the manager. 'Bring her in when you've run her a thousand miles. The first service is free.' He stepped back, waiting for Joe to take his eyes off the new possession. 'Now,' he said at length, 'if you'd like to come back to the office for the log book and cover note, you can drive her away.'

Drive her he did. Very carefully, of course, through the London traffic. Even though he had to concentrate hard on what he was doing it still seemed to him that he was riding a dream. This smart, sleek convertible—he could see its reflection in the shop windows when he pulled up at the lights—with its peppy engine and healthy exhaust, was really his own. Mr Massiter's gift to him for Christmas.

Somehow it didn't seem right to be so happy with a gift that had come from someone who'd died. And yet it had been bought for him long before, so the thought of Joe receiving it must have given some pleasure to Mr Massiter at the time. That he had thought of such a gift for Joe when he must have been feeling ill and had all the worry of the business on his mind, showed a facet of his character Joe had never suspected. It was like the money for the church. You weren't aware he'd done these things, that behind the tough business image was a very human man. It brought the sad fact home to you that so often you didn't really know someone until it was too late.

Mrs Wainwright had gone when Joe got back to the house so he didn't have to delay his announcement. He found Mrs Massiter in the library going through the letters Parker had placed on the desk.

'I've something to show you,' he said. 'Can you spare a minute?'

'What is it, Joe? Where've you been?'

'Over in Berkeley Square.' He beckoned to her. 'Come to the porch and see.'

She got up then, following him across the hall. 'What's the secret? You're so excited.'

Joe drew the front door wide.

'So would you be, Mother—with that!' He pointed to the car he'd parked at the bottom of the steps, taking further pleasure in watching her changing expression.

'What's it doing here—did you bring it?' She was looking at the car in wonder, just as he had done not an hour before.

'Yes, Mother,' he said. 'We just have to go to Bournemouth now.'

They went inside and he told her about the letter and the conversation at Brookham Garage, and she remembered then how it began.

'I'd forgotten all about it,' she said. 'And Arnold never mentioned it again. No wonder, these past weeks. But after you went back to Shelbourne in September he said he'd been thinking of getting you a car. He thought you'd worked hard at school and as you'd just passed the driving test he wanted to show his appreciation in a practical form. So he decided to buy you a car for Christmas and it was to be a special surprise.'

'It's certainly that,' Joe said. 'I still wouldn't believe it if my name wasn't on the log book—here—' He held up the folder so that she could read the name. 'See?'

She could see, but she turned away, her eyes misty.

'I'm glad you've got it, dear,' she said quietly. 'It's one thing to remember him by that they can't take away.'

Chapter Five

It was a quiet Christmas at the Pinewood Hotel. The party spirit was there, but never brash or overdone. Most of the guests were older and more subdued, though lively enough; but no one went wild or got drunk or invaded your privacy when you wanted to be alone. It was the right kind of change after a time of strain and sadness; the right kind of atmosphere to recover yourself, to get things in perspective. It brought the colour back to Mrs Massiter's face; she came out of the shadows, began to realise that life went on and you had to take advantage of that. And she was cool and sensible when she told Joe the state of affairs.

They went to church on Christmas Eve, and that was a good start. A great comfort, too. They walked to Sandbanks through the cliff-top pines on Christmas morning.

The weather was mild with bursts of hazy sunshine that flecked the grey, wrinkled plateau of the sea with sparkles of gold. Everywhere was quiet, you could tell it was Christmas Day. There was no one to see. Only the birds were about. They whistled and sang and flew noisy sorties that reminded you of Spring.

It was like Spring really, except for the patches of haze, and it was warm walking in winter clothes, especially when they were away from the trees and the sun was on them.

Mrs Massiter walked slowly which gave plenty of time to talk, but she only talked about the passing things—the hotel, the food, the guests, the peace and the view. Things like that. Nothing important. Joe thought she would take him into her confidence now. Tell him everything. Perhaps she would before they got back. But he couldn't wait any longer. What she had already said and what he had surmised only formed part of the jigsaw, there were still so many pieces missing before the picture was complete.

He would have to know soon because there were plans to make, and he already knew his first duty. It was on his mind as they walked and, during a lull in the casual conversation, he voiced his thoughts.

'I wonder what kind of job I should try and go for,' he said. 'Of course, it depends what we do—whether we stay in London.'

'Job?' Her pace slowed even more.

'Yes, I shall have to do something about it when we get home. I'm not going back to Shelbourne now.'

Her expression tensed a little.

'I hadn't thought about your leaving. You've only two terms to go. And then it was to be university. It would be such a crying shame to give up after coming so far.' Her eyes reflected her anxiety. 'I think we can manage, some how.'

'Listen, Mother, it's no use pretending. You've enough to worry you without my school fees added on. I know it's been costing nearly a hundred and fifty a term, and that's without all the personal expenses.' He looked at her with a faint, understanding smile. 'It doesn't make sense, does it? How could you do it even if I wanted it that way? And with things as I'm sure they are. There's the house to start with—we've got to leave that. What else is there?'

'I can adapt myself, Joe,' she said firmly.

'I know you can; but it's so sudden—to lose everything.' He hesitated, looking down on her from his slender height, and his voice was compassionate. 'There's nothing left for you, is there?'

'I've a little put by. Remember, I sold Valley End.'

'But that was nearly a year ago. You've been helping all along, haven't you? That's why you sold the place.'

'We never used it much, did we? It was expensive to run. There was no sense in keeping it.' A touch of nostalgia edged her voice. 'I've a little capital from that.'

'However much it is, you'll need it all now,' Joe said. 'You can't spend any more on me. It's time I took a turn. Besides, I'm not going to leave you on your own. You don't want me to leave you, do you?'

'I'm thinking what is best for you.'

'I'm grown up now. The best for me is helping you. I can start by getting a job. If you want me to I can still study. There're always evening classes. Though I don't quite know what to study for. What would you like me to do?'

'Just what offers you the best chance of being happy, dear.'

'You know what that is, Mother.'

She nodded, smiling with the memory of earlier days.

'I know. Something in the country, with animals around. Shelbourne hasn't really changed you, has it, Joe?'

'Not really. Not deep down inside.' He sighed. 'You know, I sometimes got into the country, even there. The field study centre. The botany lectures. But I knew I had to concentrate on the commercial things. And I really did, you know. For—Father's sake. I know how much he wanted me to go into the Company.'

'I know.' She spoke quietly again. 'I'm sure that was one of the reasons he died trying to save it.'

They walked on in silence for a little while and then Joe, sensing the mood, thought to change it for more hopeful things.

'Perhaps we could go down to the country, Mother,' he said. 'You like the life. And there would be heaps of jobs I could do.'

'What kind of jobs—with your education, Joe?'

'Well,' he smiled. 'Need we consider the education part? I mean, it's always good to have it, of course, but does it matter if it doesn't quite suit the job? Look at the scope in the country now. There's agriculture—I know you'd need training for that, but I'm not too old. Then there're the farm machinery agents—'

'What—selling, you mean?'

'Well, yes, that's one side of it. But there are other kinds of business. The corn and seed merchants, experimental farms both for agriculture and horticulture—I'd have to study in my spare time. And how about forestry?'

She gave him a sidelong glance, but she

didn't say anything.

'On the other hand,' he went on, wrapped in the subject, 'there are riding stables, game rearing—though I really wouldn't like that; bringing up birds to be shot for sport. But there are plenty of worthwhile things, really productive things in the country, if you go out and look for them.'

'You sound so knowledgeable, Joe,' she said at last. 'Have you been going into the prospects?'

'Not really. I just kept my ears and eyes open when I was out and about from school. I've done a lot of reading, too. Magazines and books.'

'Why? When you knew you were going for a commercial career?'

'Well, Mother,' he smiled again, 'to tell you a secret; at the back of my mind I always thought that perhaps one day—you know, in the distant future, I would get back to the country.' He paused and then, 'Now, if you were willing, the future could be quite near.'

'I don't know if that could be yet,

dear,' she said gravely. 'There will be many things to attend to in London. The lawyers like to have you near. I thought that until we see how things are going we might take on a small flat. I wondered perhaps about taking a job myself.'

'There's no need for you to do that,' Joe said, firmly. 'I'm taking the job.'

'We haven't settled anything yet,' she reminded him. 'We'll see what Mr Stringer and Mr Dawson have to say.'

Joe nodded, his eyes ranging over the placid expanse of Poole Harbour as far as the curtain of haze that veiled the hills beyond. He felt happier now. About the future. Somehow, he didn't think the country was so far away.

They went back along a quiet tree-lined road fringing the residential area. The houses were large with broad gardens, partially screened by neat hedges. There were lighted Christmas trees in windows and the sound of children's laughter. They were stable homes, secure and warm, with the smoke rising serenely from their chimneys in the pines.

They walked slowly. They had the time. And on the way she told Joe about the Company.

Arnold never talked his worries over with her, not until he was forced to seek her help. Even then she never knew the details. But she had first suspected affairs were going wrong more than a year ago. There had been some move towards a takeover, but the bid had been withdrawn. It seemed the trouble was a large office block in the Provinces which had turned out to be a complete failure. The new building appeared to have been poorly sited. Something had gone wrong with the planning. No one had wanted to buy the block or rent the offices or open the shopping parade below. Hardly anyone, that is. It was a giant empty memorial to muddled thinking on the part of all concerned. A great deal of money had gone into it, not all of it the Company's.

The Company might have survived the setback if it hadn't been for another major blunder. A site in the West End, bought freehold. The contractors moved in, demolition began; but there was one small property on the site that had been overlooked in the negotiations. And the owner refused to sell. It seemed no one could force him. So everything had stopped. And it looked like staying that way for quite a long time.

'All this I'm learning now,' she continued. 'Such a thing would never have happened if Arnold had been well. But he was ill off and on and away so much he had to leave things to Mr Rayner. Now Mr Rayner says he was only acting on Arnold's instructions.'

Joe was incensed. 'That's a dirty way of doing things—throwing all the blame on someone who's not here to deny it.'

'It seems it's all part and parcel of big business, Joe,' she said sadly. 'Arnold was the chairman, you see. And despite his flagging health he did all he could to keep the Company solvent. So much of property development, it appears, is done on borrowed money. The Insurance companies and the bank were closing in to be paid off. Reserves had already been depleted. Arnold did his best to raise new capital but no backers were forthcoming. No one would take the risks with all the complications. He tried everything to stave off disaster. I covered all our domestic expenses and he threw in all his assets. Some of his precious paintings were sold and money raised on the house; but it seems they were only drops in the ocean. You see, Joe, whatever his faults, he was an honest man, and honest men are usually the losers when they stand and fight.' She paused, a faint, helpless sigh escaping in the silence. 'Mr Dawson says Arnold was as good as bankrupt when he died.'

Joe was silent for a moment, considering his own part in the disaster.

'If only he'd told me about it,' he said softly. 'Why did he keep me at school? Why didn't he cancel the order for the car?'

'They wouldn't have made any difference.' She paused again. 'And there were other reasons, Joe. I think you can guess what they were as well as I.'

Joe could guess. Mr Massiter had treated

him as his own son. A boy at school not old enough to share the responsibilities of the adult world. It was that old paternal instinct to protect, to keep the dangers at bay. Mr Massiter had still hoped to win through, but if the worst came the gift was something salvaged from the wreck for Joe.

There was nothing he could do about it now. Nothing, that is, except the one thing he was sure Arnold Massiter would wish him to do. To take care of the woman who had mothered Joe since boyhood. And Joe was already doing that.

The interlude at Bournemouth did no end of good. Talking everything over put their problems in perspective, and although solutions would take a little time, discussing them as partners gave Joe and Mrs Massiter a mutual confidence in the future that nothing could take away.

There was a letter from Nina when they got home. It was a long letter to Joe but it included Mrs Massiter for it opened with a message of sympathy. Nina had been away in the Tyrol and had been out of touch. It wasn't until she returned to Vienna that she had heard their tragic news. She would so like to see them again, and now that she had finished her studies at the ballet school and was joining Madame Reynaud's Company in the New Year she was going to have a few days in London in between. She would stay with her Aunt Hilda in Shepherds Bush and was hoping to arrive early in January.

It was an exciting letter. Warmer than the Christmas card that arrived before they went to Bournemouth. She wanted to know how Joe was and what he was doing, but she couldn't help telling him about herself. You could see how thrilled she was to be joining the Ballet Reynaud. Her happiness oozed out of each neatly written word. Joe was happy, too. It was nice to know Nina had got what she wanted; and that he'd be seeing her again.

He wrote a short letter back saying how pleased he was to hear her good news and sent his congratulations. He ended up by asking her to post her time of arrival so that he could meet her when she came. But she didn't reply. Not by return, and there was still no news by the end of the week. The first week of January.

That was the time Mr Dawson came again. He'd spoken about Joe's future during his last visit and Joe had told him he was seeking a job. Although he hadn't mentioned it to the solicitor, he was hoping to find something in the country that would offer a cottage as well; if it wasn't too far from London he was sure Mrs Massiter would be willing to go if he could come up with a cheap and comfortable house. But it seemed that Mr Dawson had been quietly working for Joe's welfare along a different tack.

They were sitting in the library. Mrs Massiter at the desk, and the squat, watch-chained figure of the lawyer sitting in front of it, his brief case on his ample knee and files and documents neatly arrayed before him. Joe was sitting on a leather pouffe leaning back against the bookshelves.

It had been another depressing session

on a further complication concerned with Mr Massiter's estate, and Mr Dawson had gone through a rambling jargon of clauses and statistics that left the matter no clearer to Joe at the end than it had been at the beginning. All that came through was the message of which he was already aware: that Mr Massiter's personal assets and the proceeds of various shares and insurance policies would be divided amongst the creditors.

However, Mr Dawson wasn't too downhearted, and was a well of helpful advice. All along he'd been thinking that the immediate necessity was to find accommodation to relieve the expense of running the house.

'Of course, you have till the end of March,' he went on after a pause. 'So it isn't desperate, but you can't very well remain here, Mrs Massiter, without servants. I suppose they are aware of the position now?'

'Oh, yes,' she agreed. 'I told them as soon as I knew. The maid left before Christmas. But Parker and Cook want to remain until we go. They've been with us so many years.'

'Quite so.' Dawson nodded, and his double chin spread rapidly over his collar whenever he did that. 'And you can manage financially with that arrangement for the moment?'

'Yes, there's no difficulty. For the short time it will be. Mr Stringer has been looking after my personal affairs and is aware of what I am doing.'

He nodded again. 'Of course. Mr Stringer and I are in touch.' He adjusted his monocle and began shuffling the documents together. 'Naturally, having worked so closely with your late husband, I am anxious to see you have the wisest counsel. And in the matter of accommodation I took the liberty of speaking to George Gibbons.'

'Gibbons?' she frowned.

'Gibbons & Stroud, the estate agents.'

'Oh, yes, I know of them.'

'I wasn't sure whether you would be wishing to buy at the moment, but I asked him to send you particulars of any small, reasonable properties within the London area.' He glanced round at Joe, adjusting his monocle again. 'I thought if Joe was taking a job—and I'll return to that subject in a moment—you wouldn't want to be far away.'

'No,' Mrs Massiter said. 'I think it as well to be on hand until we have finally sorted everything out. But I don't want to commit myself to buying at the moment. I've been on to one or two agents about flats.'

'That's what I thought.' He was looking across the desk at her and stuffing the papers into his case. 'I asked Gibbons to include any rented properties that were suitable. He knows the position and I think he will find you something quickly.'

'That's most kind of you.'

He glanced quickly at Joe and back again.

'The school has been dealt with, I presume?' he said.

'Yes.' The word was like an apology, an admission of regret. 'Yes, Mr Stringer wrote. And Joe and I have written personally to the headmaster.'

'Well, that being settled, all we have to do now is get the boy set up in a worthwhile position.' He took a white business card from his notecase and passed it across the desk. 'I think I've found the place for him to start. It will lead to an opportunity in the professional world of which his father would have been proud.'

Joe jerked up, and moved close to the desk.

'What is it?' he asked.

'Accountancy,' Dawson said.

Joe pulled a face as Mrs Massiter handed him the card.

'But I've never been any good at figures,' he said.

'Figures are only part of it, Joe,' Dawson explained. 'There's much more to it than making a balance sheet. Company administration, legislation, management—depending on the branch of the profession in which you specialize. There are numerous opportunities right up to board level, if you're prepared to study, of course. And this little partnership,' he pointed to the card Joe held, 'will give you the chance to do that.'

Joe nodded and read the engraving: *Woodfall & Carter, Chartered Accountants, 5, Harrier's Close, London Wall, EC2.*

'Woodfall's a friend of mine,' continued the lawyer. 'He's getting on and so is his partner. They're in a small way but it is a very sound business. What they are looking for is a keen youngster who will start at the bottom and work hard, sit the exams—they'll allow time for study—and eventually take over from them. They will want to ease out, but retain an interest in the business, and they want someone reliable, trustworthy and efficient, to carry on.'

'It sounds so promising,' Mrs Massiter said. 'We're very grateful.'

Dawson beamed. His large, jovial face seemed to grow chubbier, and when he turned to look at Joe his chins rustled like tissue paper on his stiff collar and overflowed the knot of his tie.

'What does the boy say?'

'Well—thank you, sir,' Joe said. Mr

Dawson was a little like Mr Massiter for pushing you where you didn't want to go. Into a money-totting career. The commercial world, the professional world; it was all the same. Tied to a building in London, working your way up in a race to get to the top and when you finally arrived what had you to show? Power, prestige and a Rolls Royce or two, perhaps. And maybe ulcers or heart attacks or a jealous colleague waiting to knock you down. One thing you hadn't got was freedom. The freedom to do what you really wanted. You were too busy living to hold on to what you had—or dying. But, of course, he shouldn't look at things like that. Mr Dawson was only trying to help. Like Mr Massiter had done, he was only thinking of the future; what was best for Joe.

'Woodfall knows all about you,' Dawson was saying. 'There'll be no difficulties.'

'When should I get in touch, sir?' Joe asked.

'I told them you'd ring. The sooner the better. Ask for Mr Peebles. He'll make the appointment.'

'I'll do that,' Joe said. 'I'll ring them today.'

But he didn't ring. Not that day. That was the day Nina came.

Chapter Six

Nina had changed a lot since Joe last saw her. She was tall and slender with the grace and movement of some delicate yet exciting fawn-like animal. Her hair was still long and black, falling lightly about her shoulders, and her eyes were the same; wide and blue, with a kind of innocent freshness about them that reminded you of an April sky. But her face had changed a little. There was more character there; the years between the gawky school-girl and young womanhood had etched a finer contour, brought out the fullness of her lips.

Of course she'd changed. She'd grown up. So had Joe. But now she seemed older than him when he knew she was younger. He supposed she was sophisticated. That's what it was. She'd travelled a lot. Met many interesting people. She had confidence. She was doing what she wanted, and making a success of it. That made all the difference.

Mrs Massiter noticed the difference, too. And she noticed how the difference affected Joe. She thought it was a good thing for him to enjoy a little company of his own age and of the opposite sex. From her own observations Joe had never seemed to take much interest in girls. For instance, there had been the attractive girl at the Pinewood Hotel. She'd been with her family at the next table, and had had her eye on Joe. He didn't seem to notice her at all; but he was well aware of Nina. Of course they knew each other. They'd been childhood friends, if only for a brief span of time. But, even so, Joe appeared a little overwhelmed, a little bit shy. No wonder when Nina looked so feminine and glamorous. Relaxed and self-assured, too. She'd soon bring Joe round if they were left to talk alone. So Mrs Massiter left them to talk with the excuse that she was going along to the kitchen to have Cook make something dainty for tea.

'Please don't go to any trouble, Mrs Massiter,' Nina said. 'Not because of me.'

'I promise.' Mrs Massiter leaned towards her with a confidential look. 'Cook prefers to demonstrate her skill on the daintier things. She has a deft hand with sponges and gateaux, and excels at cream and chocolate fillings.'

'Oh,' Nina sighed. 'You're making my mouth water. But really I shouldn't. I love all the sweet, sugary things; but I have to be careful, especially when I'm being lazy and not practising.' She glanced down at her slender waist.

'Nonsense,' Mrs Massiter scoffed. 'You haven't any weight problems. Not at your age.'

'You'd be surprised,' Nina smiled. 'I really have to discipline myself.'

'Well, this *is* rather a special occasion,' Joe pointed out.

'Of course.' Mrs Massiter went out and closed the door.

Nina looked at Joe.

'Oh, well,' she said, smiling again, 'I'm

not going to spoil it all by arguing.' She slid out of the armchair, settling on the rug in front of the fire. 'Do you mind if I take my shoes off, Joe?'

'Of course not. Make yourself at home.'

She slipped her shoes off and curled her long shapely legs around her, leaning back against the arm of the chair.

Joe sat watching her. It was all a bit breathtaking. The way she had breezed in like that. Such a surprise, seeing her standing there when Parker opened the front door. The way she had run in to greet Joe. Throwing her arms about his neck and kissing him on the cheek. He remembered Parker turning away to hide the smile on his face. Joe hadn't known where to look or what to do with his hands. But Nina was like that. Affectionate and infectious. A little bit impetuous, decisive, not concerned with formalities. Joe must have looked awkward at the time. But she hadn't noticed.

'I hope you and your—mother didn't mind, Joe.' Nina broke into his thoughts as if she'd been reading them.

'Mind?'

'My whistling in like that, out of the blue.'

'Not likely,' Joe said. 'It was a delightful surprise. We needed cheering up, and you're just the tonic to do it. But why didn't you let me know when you were arriving? I wrote and told you I would meet you.'

'I should have written and thanked you for that.' she said apologetically. 'But everything happened so quickly; I had to change my plans and come over earlier because I'm joining Madame Reynaud's Company next week. I thought of ringing you from the airport. Then,' she paused, and there was a faintly teasing air about her, 'I decided it would be nicer to surprise you in person. So I went straight to Aunt Hilda's and left my luggage. Had lunch—and here I am.'

Joe was calculating the days.

'If you're starting the job next week, then how long are you staying in London?'

'Only till Monday, I'm afraid,' Nina said, regretfully.

'Monday?' Joe was disappointed. 'That only gives you two days.'

'I know.' She shrugged helplessly. 'But I can't help it. You see, I had no idea everything was going to happen so soon. First of all I thought I was going to have another term at school, then Madame Reynaud decided I was ready to join the Company. I think this was because an unexpected vacancy came up. Anyway, I was given leave until the twenty-fifth of this month, and as it was the first real holiday I've had for a long time, I decided to make the most of it. I went home with another pupil who lives in a snow-covered village in the Tyrol. I had a lovely time, her parents were so kind. Then, back in Vienna when I was planning my trip here, Madame Reynaud told me I must start rehearsing with the Company on the twelfth as we're going on tour at the beginning of February. You can imagine how this exciting news threw everything out.'

Joe nodded sympathetically.

'With all the things I had to do I wasn't sure whether I could even get here; but when I heard your sad news, I just wanted to come and see you. Even if it could only be a long weekend.'

'It certainly isn't long,' Joe said. 'But I'm glad you came.' He frowned, and after a moment said, 'What I can't understand is why you're not in England with an English company. I mean, there're Sadler's Wells and the Ballet Rambert—I don't know much about the ballet, but now that you've trained surely you could apply to one of the companies here?'

'Would you come and see me, Joe?'

'You know I would.'

She giggled. 'Then I could be sure of one fan.'

'Two,' he corrected. 'With Mother.'

She pressed her hands together, looking into the fire, her expression grave so that her face had almost a classical air.

'That's my ambition, to dance at Sadler's Wells,' she said wistfully. 'But as a prima ballerina. I'd like to make my debut in London as *The Sleeping Princess*. Tchaikovsky's lovely ballet.'

'Yes. I've heard of it. But how long does

it take to become a star?'

She looked round smiling. 'Who can say? It depends, on so many things. If you have talent, work hard, are lucky and get noticed, perhaps not so long.' She put her finger to her lips, reflecting. 'I hope to be well on the way by the time I'm twenty or twenty-one, perhaps.'

'So we won't see you here till then?'

'Oh, yes. I hope so. The Ballet Reynaud will be touring. All over Europe, I think. We're sure to come to London.'

'When?'

She shrugged, smiling. 'You must ask Madame Reynaud or the Tour Manager about that.'

Joe leaned forward. 'You know, I still can't see why you couldn't have begun it all in London instead of Vienna.'

She looked up, her eyes questioning.

'Don't you remember, Joe?' she asked. 'I did begin ballet classes here, and then my parents went to Austria. They had the chimpanzee act.'

'Yes, of course I remember the chimpanzees. You were touring with Farrow's Fair.'

'Yes,' she said, gazing into the fire again. 'They were happy days. Daddy and Mummy were happy. And it was fun. Or, perhaps it only seems that way when you look back on things.' Her eyes held his again. 'It was after you came out of hospital, Joe, remember? I came here once to see you.'

'I remember,' Joe nodded. 'You came to tell me how sorry you were about Smokey.'

'That must have been awful for you, Joe,' she said, softly. 'Losing Smokey, and leaving the country. The things you wanted most of all.'

'I don't think anything is lost for ever,' Joe said in a low voice, 'so long as you don't give up searching for it.' He paused, half-smiling. 'But we're talking about you.'

'And I'm afraid what I have to tell you doesn't make a very cheerful subject,' she said solemnly. 'Didn't I ever mention about my parents in a letter?'

'No. What about them?'

'They broke up,' she said, simply.

'Oh—I'm sorry,' Joe said. 'What a tragic thing.'

'It happens to people sometimes. Why does it, Joe? When they've been together a long time?' She was slowly turning the silver bracelet on her wrist. 'They joined a circus in Vienna with their act. They managed to get me an introduction to Madame Reynaud's school, and I went to classes there not only for dancing, but for general education, too. Everything seemed fine. Daddy and Mummy went on tour with the circus and I stayed in Vienna.' She paused. 'After that, I hardly saw them again.'

'What caused it all?' Joe asked, gently.

'I don't know. Mummy came back once. She said she was fed-up with the life and was getting a divorce. Daddy had some German girl. That was a year ago. I hear from them occasionally. Daddy's in Spain now. I don't think he has an act any more, but he still has this girl. And Mummy's in America. I think she's going to get married again.'

'How wretched for you,' Joe said.

'I've had to accept it. When people are grown up they make their own decisions. You can't influence their personal lives.' She raised herself on her knees, kneeling closer. 'Now, cheer up, Joe. That's enough of my role of tragedy. Tell me about you. You've been having a poor time yourself. What are your plans now?'

Joe began telling her but before he got very far, Mrs Massiter came in, followed a little later by Parker with the tea trolley.

It was very cosy sitting there, having tea and talking, with the fire roaring, and the curtains drawn, and the lamps throwing soft lights over the crumpets and the tea cakes, and cook's creamy delights on the tray. Mrs Massiter wanted to know about the ballet and Nina told her about the training, and Joe listened attentively although he'd already heard part of the story.

'The trouble is,' he announced when Nina paused to drink her cooling tea, 'she's only here till Monday. Just a long weekend, that's all.'

'What a pity,' Mrs Massiter said. And

when Nina told her why, she smiled and commented, 'Well, who'd want to miss an opportunity like that? Now, what are you going to do with the two days you're here?'

'Well,' Nina said. 'I'm staying with Aunt Hilda, and I promised to spend a little time with her. So she wants to take me down to Oxted on Sunday to see her grandchildren. But I've made no other commitments,' she added, looking at Joe.

'You can stay to dinner then?' Mrs Massiter suggested. 'Your aunt won't mind?'

'No, she's very understanding,' Nina smiled. 'But I didn't say anything about this evening. Perhaps I could ring her later.'

Joe nodded approvingly. 'And what about tomorrow?' No one answered immediately, so he went on, 'I thought, if it's a nice day—and,' he glanced at Mrs Massiter, 'if you don't want me for anything, Mother, perhaps Nina would like a drive somewhere. Say, into the country?'

'Oh,' Nina sighed. 'Could we? Have you time?'

'I think that's a splendid idea,' Mrs Massiter said. 'Choose somewhere nice, Joe, and have lunch there.'

Joe nodded happily. 'I'll think of a place.'

'That would be lovely, Joe.' Nina smiled.

Mrs Massiter glanced towards the curtained window although she couldn't see the weather outside.

'I hope it will be a nice day,' she said.

It was. Joe knew it was going to be when he went round to the Post Office to draw out ten pounds. There was no queue and the girl behind the counter was all smiles and said she hoped Arsenal would win. Joe didn't realise till afterwards that she was talking about a football match.

They went down to Marlow, and a couple of miles beyond found an old riverside inn. It was a bit noisy in the bar with the Saturday crowd, but the ingle-nook dining-room was empty. They had a table in the window overlooking the river and had lunch while the swans went by. In the afternoon they followed the winding towpath, walking an hour away in the bright sunshine that had thawed the morning frost. It was such a bright day. The sky was clear and blue, and although the breeze was cold, it was a dry, invigorating air. The grass across the water meadows was green, but on the higher levels under the trees, it glistened silver where the frost survived.

Nina was wearing a flared skirt of a faintly primrose colour, and a short fur coat in white. It wasn't an expensive fur, of course. It just looked that way on her. She looked so fresh and vibrant he could imagine her on the stage, the audience applauding; but here there was no one to see. Only the swans were looking. Eavesdropping on their conversation as they talked of many things. The past and the present and their hopes for the future. Joe could see them going their separate ways, but he knew they would never lose touch and he was proud to be her friend.

After Saturday, Sunday seemed a blank

day to Joe. With Nina at Oxted and the sun still shining and her leaving on Monday, it seemed such an awful waste. He spent the afternoon writing a letter to Aunt Ethel and Uncle Bert. They'd written to him from Australia as soon as they'd received the news. They'd written Mrs Massiter, too, and she had already replied. The letter in Aunt Ethel's handwriting was warm and sympathetic. She said they were all in the pink in Australia, but were thinking of him constantly and wondering what the future held now. Joe didn't feel like writing but he forced himself to concentrate. In the end he wrote more about Nina and didn't mention the future at all.

Monday morning's mail brought a batch of house particulars from Gibbons and Stroud. Mrs Massiter went through them over breakfast. The most likely one worth looking at was a flat in Newton Terrace, a few minutes from Marble Arch along the Bayswater Road. It was unfurnished, the rent seemed reasonable, and it was offered on a yearly tenancy.

She read the details over to Joe who was wondering where he'd put the business card Mr Dawson had given him.

'It sounds all right,' he murmured, vaguely.

'Shall we go and see it this afternoon, after you've seen Nina off?' she asked.

'Yes, if you'd like to,' Joe said. 'But I was thinking—hadn't I better ring those accountants?' He was searching his pockets. 'When I can find the card.' He looked in his notecase again.

'You were wearing your tweed jacket on Friday,' she reminded him. 'Have you looked in that?'

'No. I thought I'd put it in my wallet. I'll go up and see.'

'More coffee?'

'No thanks,' he said, as he went out.

He found the card tucked in the ticket pocket of his tweed jacket, and on the way back to the dining-room he rang Mr Peebles. He was able to fix the appointment for eleven o'clock next morning as Mr Woodfall always had Monday off.

'Good,' Mrs Massiter said when Joe

told her. 'On your way back from the airport perhaps you'll call in at Gibbons and Stroud and pick up the key?'

It was raining when they reached London Airport, and that seemed to kindle Joe's depression. He was sorry Nina was flying away. He had only had her company for a few hours but he knew how much he would miss her. All the way over to Heathrow the car echoed her gay infectious chatter. He wished she didn't sound so cheerful. It made his depression worse. But when he parked the car near Terminal One, her mood became more serious.

'Although I'm excited about everything ahead, I'm really sorry to leave, Joe,' she said softly. 'When you've settled down couldn't you fly over and see me? Say, at Easter?'

'I don't know, Nina. Depends where you'll be. You don't even know, do you?'

'Not right now. But I'll keep you posted, and maybe you'll give me the sort of surprise you said I gave you.'

Joe smiled then. He wasn't sure whether

you got more pleasure from giving or receiving.

'I was trying to think of some way to return it,' he said.

'But you've already done so really. Saturday was a lovely day.' She was looking at him, her eyes wide, and because they were so close in the car he could see where the blue of the pupils even tinged the whites.

She opened the door, then suddenly leaned back towards him.

'Thank you, Joe,' she whispered. 'For such a happy time.' She came closer and he could feel her breath. And then she kissed him.

It was a thank-you kiss. A brief demonstration of affection and friendship. Quite sisterly really. And yet, somehow, when you thought about it afterwards, not quite like that.

Chapter Seven

The flat in Newton Terrace appeared to be just the place. It was on the third floor and there was no lift, but it was light and airy, perhaps because it was nearer the sky. The Terrace was a long block of early Victorian houses that had been converted during the last decade into self-contained apartments.

Number 37A had an entrance lobby, a hall, two bedrooms, a large lounge with dining-annexe, a small kitchen and a luxury bathroom. That's how it was written in the agent's broadsheet; but compared with the bathrooms (and any other room) at Eleigh Place, it was little more than a kitchen sink. How Mrs Massiter was going to adapt herself Joe couldn't imagine, but he knew that she would.

It looked as if the last tenant had moved out very recently for you could see the freshly scarred paintwork on two of the doorways where the removal men had carelessly scraped some items of furniture; but on the whole the flat was in good condition and the decorators had been in not many weeks before.

It didn't take long to view. Joe followed Mrs Massiter through all the rooms and when they returned to the lounge, she paused near the window, slowly examining the room again, obviously considering how best to set out some of the furniture she was retaining. He knew she had listed the items she planned to keep from the vast collection of furnishings at Eleigh Place, and what she couldn't use in their new home would be put in store. The remainder was to be sold, and Mr Stringer was looking after that.

'Well, Joe?' she said at last, moving to the centre of the room. 'What do you think?'

'Yes, I like it,' he nodded.

'It's nicely arranged and large enough for the two of us, though it would have been more convenient to have had another bedroom.'

'Well, we can manage. It's only going to be temporary,' Joe reminded her. 'For the year, anyway.'

'Of course,' she said. 'And all other conditions being what they are, I think we ought to take it before someone else steps in.' Her eyes were roving again and he could tell by the look in them that she was already visualising herself living there. The flat represented the final break with the old world; it was a turning point, a future that offered challenge and new interests just because it was so different. That would account for the expression in her eyes.

'Are you satisfied?' She moved towards him. 'You can't see any snags?'

'No. It looks fine to me.' He turned towards the hall, and that was the moment he noticed the cupboard.

It was small, low, with two doors, no more than two feet from the floor in depth. It fitted flush into a recess in the wall which made it unobtrusive. It probably housed the electric meter and would take only the smaller domestic items. It must have been the one place in the flat they hadn't examined. Joe certainly had not noticed that one of the doors was slightly open; and now, to his astonishment, it opened still further—a very slow movement as if something inside was pressing gently against it. As he stepped forward curiously, a small furry head appeared followed by a tortoiseshell body. He couldn't believe his eyes as he stared at the little creature, which looked up at him and opened its mouth in a faint plaintive cry.

He moved carefully out into the hall, stooping low and calling softly, 'Mother, come and look! We already have a tenant. Just come and see this kitten.'

'Kitten!' Mrs Massiter exclaimed, hurrying to join him in the hall.

'What a surprise!' Joe had already scooped up the bundle of fur and was holding the kitten against his chest. The creature began to purr and climbed higher, nestling under Joe's chin.

'How sweet.' Mrs Massiter warmed to the little animal, but looked highly confused by its presence there. 'Where did he come from, Joe?'

Joe nodded towards the open cupboard. 'And I don't think it's a boy. I believe it's very rare to find a male tortoiseshell.' He gently turned the kitten over, and the creature thought it a game which gave her an opportunity to kick her legs and nibble Joe's fingers. Joe didn't mind. He looked up smiling. 'Yes,' he said confidently, 'she's a girl all right. Three or four months old, I should say.'

Mrs Massiter was peering into the cupboard as if afraid she might find more, but apart from the electricity meter and the fuse box there was only an old attache case without its lid, containing a couple of faded yellow dusters.

'Look, here's where she settled,' Mrs Massiter said.

Joe nodded. The kitten purred louder, climbed on to his shoulder and started to wash his neck.

'She's taken a fancy to you,' Mrs Massiter said. 'But what are we going to do with her?'

'Do?' Joe repeated, surprised. 'Well,

obviously we can't leave her here, Mother. We shall have to take her home.' He was stroking the soft fur. The coat was silky to the touch, and the colour markings of fawn, brown, dark brown and white made up a pretty but indeterminate pattern. There were streaks of orange and black here and there and a heart-shaped bib of white under the chin. On one side of the neat pink nose the face was a light fawn colour and on the other changed dramatically to walnut brown. The whiskers were white, long and straight.

Mrs Massiter smiled. She remembered Joe and his animals. He hadn't had a pet since he was a boy at Valley End—Smokey had been the last. She could see how the kitten affected him, and she sympathised. She didn't want to upset him by pointing out the truth of the situation too brashly, but it had to be done.

'What I mean is, dear,' she said, gently, 'she looks well cared for so she must be someone's pet. We can't just take her over without checking. Perhaps she belongs to the last tenant; they could have moved out a few days ago and somehow overlooked her.'

'In that case,' Joe said, firmly, 'they don't deserve to have her.'

'That doesn't alter the fact of ownership. They may be sending for her now. I'm afraid I must ask the agent.'

Joe was frowning, seeking another, less binding explanation.

'Of course,' he said at last, 'she might be a stray.'

'Then how did she get in? I didn't see a window open, did you?'

'No. I didn't notice. But how many people have been in to view? Don't you see, Mother, one of them could have left the front door open while they were looking round. You know how curious cats are. She could have just walked in and settled in the cupboard.'

Mrs Massiter put her finger to her lips. She did that sometimes when she was reflecting.

'In that case, Joe,' she said, 'she might have strayed from one of the neighbouring flats. I think we ought to enquire.'

'What—now, you mean?' He looked disappointed.

'Well, yes, don't you think so, before we take her away?'

'All right,' he admitted, with reluctant resignation. 'You sit in the car with the kitten, and I'll make the enquiries.'

It took nearly twenty minutes to make the round, and just to please Mrs Massiter Joe called at the flats on either side as well as the two below 37A. When he returned Mrs Massiter could tell by the grin on his face that none of them owned a kitten.

'Well,' he said, getting into the car, 'I think that stakes our claim. No one even owns a cat let alone a tortoiseshell kitten.'

They didn't get back to Eleigh Place until after five. Joe insisted on finding a pet shop, and when they found one, he bought a cat basket, a tin of cat food, a bag of pet litter and a toilet tray.

'Even if the owner did turn up,' he explained slyly, 'the equipment will always come in useful for the future.'

There was no reply from the house

agents when Mrs Massiter rang, and she realised the office had closed for the day. She found Joe in the lounge playing with the kitten on the rug in front of the fire, and told him she couldn't get through.

'I'll ring them at nine in the morning,' she continued, 'and tell them we'll take the flat. I'll have to mention the kitten, so don't get too fond of her, Joe; I hope we can keep her, but it's just possible the late tenants may want her back.'

Joe smiled up at her, nodding.

'I'll try and remain neutral,' he said.

The kitten spent the night in the box-room at the further end of the landing. Joe put her basket near the radiator, left a saucer of warm milk, and demonstrated the reason for the tray by firmly placing her in it. She kept getting out and he kept putting her back until eventually the penny dropped. He went to bed then, smiling. He thought she was going to be a very intelligent cat.

Mrs Massiter rang the agents soon after nine next morning whilst Joe was finishing his breakfast. The kitten sat on his lap, her eyes just above the table top, following his every movement. Although she had been fed she was still willing to accept every morsel he offered her from his plate, and there was no denying she now considered herself a member of the family.

When Parker came in for the breakfast trolley Joe pushed his plate away and moved on to the rug where the kitten began to give an acrobatic display as Joe swung the ping-pong ball, which he'd threaded on a piece of string, round and round her head.

Parker stood and watched, his expression one of benevolent amusement. He'd never been one for animals, but he would have to admit, if pressed, that the kitten came as near as anything could to changing his mind.

'She's a pretty little thing, Mr Joe,' he said. 'Settled down by the look of it, too. I hope you'll be able to keep her.'

'If anyone tries to claim her now, they'll have to give me proof of ownership.' Joe rolled the kitten over and she suddenly sat up and scratched an ear, then relaxed to begin a washing session.

'What are you going to call her?' Parker enquired.

Joe stared from Parker to the subject on the floor and back to the old man again.

'Well...can you beat that!' He seemed to have surprised himself. 'She's been in the house since last night and I hadn't thought about a name.'

Parker smiled. 'If I may say so, sir, that shouldn't be so extraordinary. After all, as madam says, you couldn't be absolutely certain as to the creature's future whereabouts.'

'Her whereabouts are here,' Joe said firmly. 'I'm not going to consider improbabilities. I'm going to consider a name. Now, it must be something different. Can you think of anything?'

Parker studied his immaculate cuffs as if the answer was written there.

'It's not easy on the spur of the moment, Mr Joe,' he said at length, 'to think of something different.'

Joe agreed, and mentally began a run-through of the names of all the pets he'd had...Smokey—well, of course, that was a very special name. Then there was Tinker...Amber...Caution...Nutmeg... Alfie... But it didn't seem right to use one of those. Each animal had had their own individual character, and no new arrival could take their place. Besides, the kitten was so different from any pet he'd had before, so she warranted something unusual. But he couldn't think of anything at the moment.

It looked as if Parker had. Thought of something, that is. He cleared his throat.

'What about a day of the week, Mr Joe?' he suggested brightly.

'You mean—what day of the week is it?'

'No. One of the days of the week. I mean—well, take today.'

'What about it?'

'Well, it's Tuesday, isn't it?'

'Yes, of course it is.'

'Well, sir, that's it, if I may say so. It's different.'

'*Tuesday*—I see—of course!' Joe laughed at his own confusion. 'That's a splendid name. I must be dense this morning not to have caught on in the first place. Yes, I like it...I'm sure Mother will.' He gazed down at the kitten who had now curled herself into a ball. 'Tuesday...' It rolled off the tongue, and somehow seemed to go with her tortoiseshell coat. He smiled at the old man. 'Thank you, Parker,' he said. 'I think we'll settle for that.'

When Mrs Massiter came in and announced she had arranged to take the flat, Joe wanted to know about the late tenants.

'They moved out on Friday,' she said. 'And they're going abroad. The agent knows nothing about a kitten, but he told me someone was in looking round the flat on Saturday morning. Apparently they turned it down.' She was looking at the kitten. 'I can't believe the tenants were heartless enough to leave her there.'

'You'd be surprised what some people do,' Joe said. 'But she might have got in unnoticed on Saturday morning.'

'Either way,' Mrs Massiter smiled, 'she's

landed on her four feet now. She's yours, Joe.'

They all looked relieved, including Parker. But Tuesday didn't disturb herself. It seemed she'd never harboured any doubts all along.

At five minutes to eleven Joe found a vacant meter a few yards from Harrier's Close so there was plenty of time to locate Number 5. He found Woodfall and Carter on the first floor and was shown into the office of the senior partner. Mr Carter joined them a few moments later. The partners were both getting on in years and, like the office furniture, were a bit old-fashioned. They had the appearance of benevolent city gentlemen in their pin-stripe suits, reminding Joe of old engravings he had seen of city merchants in their top hats. But he couldn't see any top hats on the clothes stand in the corner.

They were rather alike in appearance. Both were tall and thin with sallow faces and scraggy necks tortured by high stiff collars. The only difference between them was a pair of glasses and a head of hair.

Mr Woodfall had the hair, frail and silvery; Mr Carter had no hair on his head at all; it was mostly in his eyebrows which were thick and bushy, overhanging his gold-rimmed spectacles. They spoke in soft, polite voices, and Mr Woodfall did most of the talking.

He was very sympathetic about Joe's personal bereavement and considered the loss of Winthrop Property Developments a tragedy for the property world. Mr Carter seemed to bow his head in sympathy, but he perked up when his partner got on to more cheerful things. Mr Woodfall asked Joe about Shelbourne, and nodded approvingly when Joe modestly listed his qualifications. They both thought Joe had had an advantageous start. Mr Woodfall then went on to explain the terms of service.

It seemed like a long stint to Joe. Five years working as a kind of apprentice, split in the middle with an intermediate exam and two separate examinations to obtain his Final by the end of the fifth year. His daily attendance at the office and the studies in his spare time weren't going to give him a moment to do anything else. But as things were, he thought he should consider himself lucky. It was his first job. And he was learning a profession and being offered a salary that would make him independent at the same time.

Mr Woodfall seemed satisfied as he brought the interview to a close, but he wanted confirmation from his partner.

'I think we've covered everything,' he said, with a glance at Mr Carter. 'Have you any further questions, Harold?'

'I don't think so,' Mr Carter said slowly. 'Except the question of the day of commencement.' He was looking at Joe. 'When would it be convenient for you to join us?'

'I'm free to start at any time, sir,' Joe said.

'Excellent,' said Mr Woodfall. 'Then shall we say next Monday?'

'Nine o'clock,' added Mr Carter, precisely.

His partner nodded, giving Joe a welcome look.

'Now, we'll just have Mr Peebles show you round,' he said.

There wasn't much to see. It was a small suite of offices on the first floor. The building was very old and the rooms were small with not much daylight. Mr Peebles seemed very much at home there. He was younger than the partners, but not much younger, and he had obviously grown old with the place and now considered himself a natural part of it.

After looking into a couple of rooms and introducing Joe to some of the staff, Mr Peebles led him back through the small general office and along a narrow corridor. He pointed out his own office and stopped at the door just beyond. It was the last one, anyway. He opened the door.

'This will be your office,' he said, inviting Joe to step in. 'I'm afraid it isn't very large and it needs tidying up, but I'll have it presentable by Monday.' He had a high-pitched voice, and although he spoke with hopeful encouragement, his eyes looked tired and dull behind the horn-rimmed glasses; but this impression may have been due to the light. Very little seeped into the room through the small square window. The desk was covered with boxes of stationery, and there were files all over the place as well as a couple of packing cases in the corner. 'I regret to say the junior staff have been treating it as a kind of general store,' he went on, blinking his apologies. 'But we'll soon have it straightened out. There are one or two pieces to come in—a desk lamp, a cabinet and a chair. You won't know it on Monday.'

Joe said he was sure he wouldn't, and went to the desk. The window was opposite and set rather high in the wall. Looking through it across the desk the view wasn't very inspiring. Harrier's Close appeared to widen out at the end of the building, but not enough to improve the view. Joe's window overlooked the Close from the end of the block, and the adjoining buildings rose high on either side until the narrow avenue turned at right angles to a tall brick wall. Beyond the wall two new skyscraper blocks shut out all else except a slim oblong of sky. It was a depressing aspect really, when you thought about the country, and the sky at that moment looked as grey and cold as Joe felt.

On the other hand, Mr Peebles didn't seem to notice the window nor appear to care what was outside. Joe thought he wouldn't even notice if there'd been no window at all. The man went on talking and gesturing like some tourist guide until eventually Joe edged into the corridor and apologised for taking up so much of his time. He was able to get away then; but he didn't look forward to Monday.

He cheered himself up a little on the drive back to Eleigh Place. It might not be so bad. And they were nice people. It was quiet there, and the atmosphere and the pace gave the impression of a partnership with Time; not a race against it. Besides, he had to have a job. And one with professional prospects was better than any. How could you argue with that?

Mrs Massiter wanted to know all about it when Joe got home. They sat in the lounge and he told her while Tuesday played with the lace of his shoe.

'Congratulations, dear,' Mrs Massiter said when he had fully reported and answered all her questions. 'It was kind of Mr Dawson to speak for you. And whatever you do later on, Joe, a qualification like that will always be of use.'

He smiled faintly.

'That's how I look at it,' he said.

Mrs Massiter glanced at the clock, and rose from her chair.

'I'd better see Cook,' she announced. 'Vincent's coming for lunch.'

'Sir Vincent Craig?'

'Yes. He rang a little while ago. He wanted to know if we'd found accommodation.'

'You told him about the flat?'

'Yes.'

'What did he say?'

'Advised me not to finalise it yet.'

'Why ever not?'

'He said an unusual opportunity had come up through a friend of his, and he'd like to talk it over. So I suggested he come round for lunch.'

'Opportunity?' Joe stopped tickling Tuesday's ears. He looked distinctly puzzled. 'Some kind of job apparently.'

'Job? But didn't you tell him I'd already—'

'No, dear,' she interrupted gently. 'Not a job for you.' There was a faint flush in her cheeks now. 'For me.'

Chapter Eight

Mrs Massiter had to admit the idea appealed to her. It was so completely different to her old life and a great deal more exciting than the new level of living she had visualized for herself in the flat in Newton Terrace. Sir Vincent's argument in favour would have been that of any good psychologist. She could see how sensible it was. She was still young, in the middle years; active, needing something to fill the void created in the loss of all she had known before. It would be a challenge. Something to occupy her mind and energies all day and every day. But she had never really been exposed to the commercial world; never held a job in her life. Not a serious job. She wasn't sure that she could do it. She wasn't sure Joe would want her to do it. She had to consider him. She knew how much he considered her.

'I hardly know what to say, Vincent,' she spoke at last. 'I've no experience. It needs someone who is acquainted with the business.'

'Nonsense, Laura,' Sir Vincent said gently in his soft, mild voice. 'It needs someone with tact, poise, personality and good sense. You have those things. And I'm sure you would have a flair for it because your family were in the hotel business, weren't they?'

'Yes. But I'm afraid I didn't do very much in it. Not seriously.'

'There,' he said blandly, 'doesn't Life work our moves out for us? Not always so conveniently,' he added with a smile. 'But it is quite obvious, Laura, you would take this situation in your stride. I think you will find you'll need something.'

'There're always opportunities for social work.'

'Of course there are, but can you afford to be so benevolent just at the present time? Besides, you need a challenge. Something more demanding. In any event, I can't see you wasting yourself away cooped up in a flat. Imagine it!' He glanced at Joe as if seeking approval.

Mrs Massiter glanced at him, too.

'You haven't said anything, dear,' she reminded him. 'What do you think about it?'

Joe stirred his coffee again. He didn't like the idea of it at all. Apart from his reluctance to see her tied to a job he saw it as another obstacle across their path to the country. It was bad enough his being bound to a desk in the City; if she became involved in the running of a successful hotel what were the prospects of ever getting away? The position, too, put him off. A kind of hostess. It sounded more like something in a night club. Of course, he knew it wasn't like that. Sir Vincent would hardly suggest anything for Mrs Massiter that wasn't ladylike, proper, and in good taste. He was only thinking of her welfare. Joe hadn't stopped to consider just how much living in a small flat might mean. After a time, what effect might it have on her. A continual fight against boredom, he could see that now. Of course she would want something to do. If it would make her happy to take on such a job, what justification had he to object? He'd been looking at it from his point of view. Selfishly. And that wouldn't do.

He smiled across the table at her.

'I thought I was the one who was going to work,' he said. 'But if it's what you want, Mother, I'll help you all I can.'

Mrs Massiter looked at him reminding herself that she must not forget what *he* wanted. She felt within her that somehow the steps they were considering now might lead them there in the end.

'Joe would really like to go back to the country, Vincent,' she said, her eyes smiling at their guest.

He nodded, leaning back in the chair, comfortably fed, thoughtfully drawing on his cigar, his soft voice enhancing his dignified appearance.

'If that's what you would both like to do there's no need to rule it out,' he said. 'I see this as an opportunity to get you back on your feet, Laura. A tonic to bridge you over the gap I know you have to cross.

It hasn't got to last for ever, but while Joe is in London it would be convenient in many ways, surely? Moreover, Jefferson might well decide to expand, and why not in the direction of the country? I shouldn't be at all surprised if he bought the Falcon Hotel at Bidhurst in Dorset. He told me it was likely to come on the market in the autumn.'

'But this one in Knightsbridge,' Mrs Massiter said. 'What kind of place is it, and what does he want to do there?'

'Well, of course, it's a small hotel in Welgar Street.' Sir Vincent pushed his coffee cup aside and moved the ashtray nearer. 'The Marlborough—did I mention the name? I don't think he wants to enlarge it. Just improve it. It's very English apparently—food, atmosphere and so forth, and consequently most of the clientele are overseas visitors, particularly Americans. Although it is running smoothly enough under the manager, Jefferson feels it lacks something. He wouldn't want to change the staff; just bring someone in who could improve an already excellent service.

Normally the manager's wife would provide the woman's touch, but this man is a bachelor. So they need someone who could give that little extra care and attention to the guests. A hostess, no more, no less.'

'It doesn't sound a very difficult assignment,' Mrs Massiter declared.

'Certainly not for you, Laura. You see,' Sir Vincent stubbed his cigar into the ashtray, 'Jefferson feels there is not sufficient personal attention given, especially in the smaller hotels, and while he doesn't consider it should be obtrusive he is convinced it is a service that should be there. He was airing his thoughts on the subject on Saturday evening at dinner when he mentioned he was looking for someone for the Marlborough.'

'Is it one of a group?' Mrs Massiter asked.

'No. It's Jefferson's first venture into the catering industry. But he is keen. He may expand. He's a very successful old friend of mine with many strings to his bow. He usually takes my advice professionally, and sometimes in other spheres.' Sir Vincent smiled. 'That's why I mentioned you. And he'd like to meet you.'

She looked a little anxious. 'You didn't tell him I was seeking a job?'

'No, my dear.' His smile was even more relaxed. 'I just mentioned some of your qualities, and that you were a friend of mine.'

There was a pause while Mrs Massiter replenished the three cups with coffee, and Joe, who had listened attentively for so long, was anxious to ask a question or two himself.

'I suppose we should be living there, sir?' he said.

'You would, of course, have that option,' Sir Vincent nodded. 'And in the circumstances it would suit your situation admirably. I'm sure the private quarters would be comfortable.'

'And there'd be no objection to taking Tuesday?' Joe persisted.

Mrs Massiter set down the Cona and smiled at their guest's faintly bewildered expression.

'Tuesday is Joe's kitten,' she explained

quickly. 'She's just joined the family.'

'Ah, I see.' Sir Vincent's lean face wrinkled with laughter lines. 'No, I'm sure there would be no objection to a cat. As a matter of fact, I think the manager has some kind of pet himself.'

Joe nodded. He felt a little more relieved now, and wondered what kind of pet the manager had.

Mrs Massiter sat down again and brought the conversation back to a more immediate question.

'I assume there is a little time to consider it all?' she said.

'Naturally, you will want to think it over. I told Jefferson I would let him know this week, and, if you are interested, he'll ring you. Now,' he leaned back, clasping his hands together as if he were giving some professional advice to a patient, 'why not go and see the place first? You must know what it's like before you can begin to make up your mind. Why don't you both have lunch there tomorrow?'

And that's what they did.

Welgar Street was a quiet avenue, and

the portico entrance of the Marlborough Hotel, a couple of hundred yards from the corner where the street spilled into Knightsbridge, made a bright promontory amidst the rather dull surroundings. Situated in the centre of a long block, the hotel was easily recognised by the face-lift it had recently undergone.

Up the steps and through the swing doors brought you into a broad reception hall with a staircase of red carpet circling an old-fashioned lift shaft opposite the entrance. On one side was an archway opening on to a bar, on the other a small lounge. Here an aisle flanked the mirrored wall, and at the end were the glass doors leading to the restaurant.

Mrs Massiter had telephoned about a table, and a waiter led them to one in the window. He gave them a menu each and asked if they would like a drink. Mrs Massiter ordered a Campari and Joe had a light sherry, and they studied the menu. There was a wide selection of savouries and soups and the usual choice of juices, but the main course was rather limited.

It was a cold day so they had asparagus soup, and Mrs Massiter chose Norfolk duckling to follow. Joe had Shepherd's Pie. It was easy to eat and didn't require any awkward fiddling with knife and fork, so he could concentrate on observing the surroundings.

There was nothing particularly notable about them. The restaurant was not large, seating no more than fifty people, and about half that number were dining, although a few were still drifting in. The room had a high patterned ceiling with hanging clusters of lights, and a mild decor that emphasized the impression of spaciousness. The face-lift outside had increased the daylight inside because the windows appeared to have been entirely reconstructed. They were tall and wide and draped with thick velvet curtains in a shade that matched the dark red carpet. Like the menu, everything in the room appeared to strike an English note.

Mrs Massiter touched her lips with her table napkin, and eyed Joe. Over the three courses they had discussed their observations but had not yet summed up their conclusions.

'Well, Joe,' she said, 'what do you think? Can you see yourself living here?'

Joe smiled. 'Not actually in *here*. I suppose we could eat in our own private room or rooms, wherever they are.'

'I'm sure we'd have that choice,' she said. 'Of course, so much depends on what the accommodation is like, what kind of man the manager is, and what my exact duties would be. None of these things can be ascertained till I meet Mr Jefferson and he gives me an official introduction here.'

Joe nodded. 'I can't see that we're going to find out much today.'

'That wasn't the purpose of the visit. We only came for a first impression.'

'Well, assuming all the others things are favourable,' he said, 'how do you feel about it?'

Mrs Massiter was silent for a moment, looking around again as the waiter served the coffee.

'I don't know,' she said slowly, when the man had gone. 'I don't know that I could do it. Yet, the whole idea intrigues me. It's a challenge. Something entirely new.'

'You could do it, Mother,' Joe said with pride. 'You could make a success of anything you made up your mind to do. But doing a job is one thing; living with it is another.'

She didn't say anything to that, and he went on, 'What I mean is, if working and living here means you are going to be on call twenty-four hours a day then you've got to be very happy with the work. It's like having your own business, you never get away from it, and that's fine if you are doing what you want to do, but if you aren't happy, well...'

'If I took it on I should want some privacy and regular periods of time to myself. No one would expect any more or any less than that. And I wouldn't commit myself by signing any long-running contract. You can safely leave that to me,' she added with a smile.

'Yes,' he said, wryly, 'I'm sure I can.'

Outside in the reception hall Joe paused, waiting for Mrs Massiter to collect her coat. At the end of a short corridor in line with the reception desk he noticed a door with the manager's name on it, but there was no sign of anyone who looked like him.

As they went down the steps Joe told her the manager's name was Sopwith. 'I wonder what kind of animal he has?' he murmured. 'I mean, living in an hotel, he couldn't have anything larger than a cat or a lap dog, could he?'

'I don't know, dear,' she said. 'Perhaps he has a canary. I'll find out for you.'

Joe gave her a sidelong glance.

'You've made up your mind, then?' he suggested quietly, opening the door of the car.

She ducked under the hood and into the passenger seat so he didn't see her smile.

'I've made up my mind to see Jefferson,' she said.

That evening she telephoned Sir Vincent Craig and he said he would contact Laurence Jefferson. On Wednesday the draft agreement for the flat arrived from Gibbons and Stroud and she sent it on to Mr Stringer explaining her intention of deferring the negotiations for a few days. On Thursday Joe heard from Nina; but it was not until Friday that Mr Jefferson rang, inviting Mrs Massiter to lunch with him the following Monday.

And so the week slipped by and on Monday morning Joe was ready to leave for the City at eight-thirty. Mrs Massiter looked him over and liked what she saw. She brushed an imaginary hair from his collar and straightened the knot of his tie.

'Good luck, dear,' she said.

'Good luck to you, Mother, too,' Joe smiled, and his smile spread to her as each caught the mood of the unusual moment that was starting them on their first but separate ventures.

'What time did you say your appointment was?' he asked.

'Twelve o'clock, at his office in Park Lane.'

'Well, don't forget to put Tuesday in her room before you go,' Joe said, anxious lest Parker or Cook should accidentally let the kitten out. 'I've left everything ready.

And then whoever's back first can bring her down.'

Joe was back first. He was surprised really, because it was almost six o'clock, and however sumptuous the lunch Mr Jefferson had given Mrs Massiter, it would hardly last the whole afternoon. He brought Tuesday down to the lounge, the creature still yawning in his arms, and after a saucer of milk and fish, she curled up in her basket beside the fire and went to sleep again.

Joe lay back, too, in the deep armchair, munching a biscuit and helping himself from the pot of tea which Parker had thoughtfully left for him while he was upstairs. It hadn't been a very interesting day. He'd done nothing of any note at all. But then he supposed first days in a new job were like that. He hadn't even seen the partners. Mr Peebles had introduced him to two members of the staff Joe hadn't met on his first visit to the office, showed him how to use the small telephone switchboard in case he ever had to fill-in while the junior was away, and explained the routine for the mail. He'd had a look at the filing system, and Mr Peebles had shown him some of the books that would come to him for checking once he was well and truly settled in. The small office allotted to Joe had been tidied up and even the window had been cleaned; you could see where the duster had smeared a cobweb in the corner. But Joe had spent most of the time with Mr Peebles, and the only moments he had sat at his own desk was when the girl came round with the tea. Still, he'd started, that was the main thing and, looking at it from the point of view of his real ambition, it was a depressing thing, too.

He pushed the tea tray aside and wandered about the room, wondering how Mrs Massiter had fared, and a few moments later, just when he was looking at the clock again, he heard her in the hall. He opened the lounge door and she came in smiling, her face pale where the cold wind had nipped it. She sat down, warming her hands by the fire, asking all the questions, but before Joe could answer one, Parker appeared with another tray of tea. While Joe served her he talked about his day. There wasn't much to tell, and he was impatient to know what she had done and why she was away so long.

'So you see,' he ended, when she could think of no more questions, 'nothing much happened to me. But how about you?' He noticed how bright her eyes were, how youthful the smile, how the flush of colour creeping back into her cheeks, seemed to have ironed away the faint lines the past months had carved there. 'Did you lunch at the Marlborough?'

'No,' she said. 'The Dorchester, but we went on to Knightsbridge afterwards. And we've been at the Marlborough the whole afternoon.'

'So you're going to take the job?'

She was drinking tea so she couldn't reply immediately, but even if she hadn't nodded, the answer was there in her face.

'I couldn't resist it, Joe,' she said, putting down the cup and saucer. 'I think it's going to be an interesting and stimulating exercise. And there's nothing to bind us down. Mr Jefferson is a most charming

143

man. I don't know what Vincent told him, but he went out of his way to assure me that if I found it unsuitable or I was unhappy after giving it all a fair trial, he would assist all he could in whatever I planned to do.'

'Well, that's reasonable,' Joe said.

'And we've our own private suite on the top floor.' She paused, reflecting. 'H'm, fourth, I think that is. And really, dear, it's larger than the flat in Newton Terrace. Nicely furnished, too, and all ready for occupation. So we'll have to put the furniture we were going to take with us in store with the rest.'

'There'll be room for our personal things?' Joe queried. 'I've quite a number, and I'd want somewhere to hang that picture of Smokey.'

'Of course,' she agreed. 'It's not over-crowded. You'll have space enough for what you want. Mr Sopwith appears to have furnished his own little flatlet. It was more in period style so I assumed it was his personal choice. His rooms are on the same floor and Mr Jefferson and I joined him there for a drink. He's a rather shy man, older than I expected, but I'm sure he'll be very easy to get along with.'

'Did he seem the type who's fond of animals?' Joe gave her a teasing look. 'You know I'm really waiting for you to tell me what kind of pet he has.'

She put her hand to her mouth. 'I'm sure you won't appreciate this, dear, but I was so taken up with everything I completely forgot to ask. But, of course, I saw it. Some kind of cage bird.' She frowned.

'Not a budgerigar?'

'Oh, no. Quite different. A larger bird, almost the size of a rook, with black plumage, yellowy beak, legs and feet. I ought to know the name though I don't think I've seen one before.'

Joe was listening intently. 'Did it talk?'

'No. At least, not for the moment I saw it. Mr Sopwith took it into another room.'

'He probably thought it might say something it shouldn't, with Mr Jefferson there,' Joe smiled. 'It sounds like a Mynah bird to me. They talk a lot.' He glanced down at Tuesday still asleep in the basket. 'Did you tell him we had a cat?'

'I mentioned it to Mr Jefferson, but didn't get a chance to tell the manager.'

'Well, if the bird is very tame he probably lets it fly around.'

Mrs Massiter looked anxiously at the kitten, then back to Joe. 'Not outside his own rooms surely?'

Joe shrugged.

'I shouldn't think so,' he said. 'But we'll have to keep an eye on Tuesday.'

Chapter Nine

They moved out of Eleigh Place at the beginning of February. It was snowing in the morning although as the day wore on the sky opened a little and a weak sun came through. Soon the snow began thawing, and the streets were clear, glistening wet in the sunlight that melted away the slush in the gutters.

The weather didn't make much difference. It wasn't a full scale move. Just a small van to take the personal things. All the furniture Mrs Massiter was keeping had gone into store the previous day. The rest was coming up for auction the following week, and Mr Stringer had set up everything for that.

Mr Woodfall had given Joe the day off, and Joe had made three trips in the car with a variety of cases containing some of his and Mrs Massiter's more precious things that they didn't want to chance with the vanman. Like the picture of Smokey which had travelled carefully wrapped on the back seat, and Tuesday in the basket in the front.

It was sad leaving the house, but Joe knew it was a greater parting for Mrs Massiter. It had been her elegant home for so long, whereas Joe had lived most of his growing years away at school. But the saddest moment of all was saying goodbye to Parker.

Parker and Cook were leaving together but they were going separate ways. Perhaps it wasn't so bad for Mrs Flowers. She was adaptable, easy-going, and on the right side of fifty; plump and jolly, nothing seemed to get under her Yorkshire skin. Although she was sorry to be leaving Mrs Massiter in such unfortunate circumstances, you could see she thought the job in the Worthing hotel would be a nice change, and if that wasn't enough there was the cheque Mrs Massiter gave her to help her on the way.

Parker was different. He was older,

closer to retiring, and had always been in domestic service. He'd served the household for so many years he'd never thought of going away. He was proud of his position, had been so attached to the family he didn't want to leave Mrs Massiter now. You could see how much he felt it when he said goodbye for he said it with a bouquet of flowers. Spring flowers, they were. A token of respect and a promise of happier days to come.

Mrs Massiter was deeply touched. Her feelings were in her voice when she thanked him for his loyal service. She thought he had earned his retirement and she was glad to know that he was going to stay with his widowed sister in Gloucester.

Joe said he was glad, too, and he hoped Parker would be happy there. He waited till Mrs Massiter had given Parker her parting gift, then followed with his own.

Settling in at the Marlborough didn't take as long as Joe had feared. He liked their suite and the novelty of living in an hotel. He got on well with Mr Sopwith. Especially when he told the man of his weakness for animals, and talked about his early days in the country. Mr Sopwith liked the country, too, but he never seemed to find the time to go there. Only in his holidays, when a relief manager came in. He was keen on ornithology, as Joe had guessed by the books on the subject he'd noticed when he had first visited the manager's rooms.

So Joe could understand about Percy. The Mynah bird. Mr Sopwith thought the world of him. You could appreciate that, Mr Sopwith being a bachelor. It was nice to have a friend to talk to sometimes when you were alone. Percy could talk back, too. Mr Sopwith had trained him from the age of three months. But you had to be careful. He was still not a year old and would pick up and repeat anything that was said. After that age, Joe learned, the bird would seldom say anything new; his vocal development and training took place mostly in the first year.

'He likes the television,' Mr Sopwith told Joe one day when Percy was out of his cage and perched on his master's shoulder. 'So you have to be careful what programmes he views. Those plays they put on, for instance; it wouldn't do for him to hear some of the things that are said. Fortunately, they usually come on late, and if I want to look in, Percy's in bed.'

Joe nodded. He understood. But he hadn't heard Percy talk much and was keen to set him off, so he got Mr Sopwith's permission and fixed the bird with a steady eye.

'What time do you go to bed?' Joe spoke very distinctly, but Percy said nothing; just sat and ruffled his feathers. Joe took a quick breath and repeated the question, speaking slowly in a deeper voice.

The bird reacted immediately. 'What time do you go to bed?' The voice mimicked Joe's slow deep tone, and then, in higher pitch, 'Why don't you grow up.'

Joe was surprised and amused. Mr Sopwith smiled, too, as he put Percy back in the cage.

'That was an expression he picked up

from TV,' he said. 'Mynahs are great imitators. You see how careful one has to be?'

Joe heard other samples from Percy's repertoire over the weeks, and was often tempted to call at the suite along the corridor but refrained from doing so for fear of making himself a nuisance. Besides, he had Tuesday to exercise. Sometimes he would do this on the top landings, sometimes in the yard at the back of the hotel.

As Tuesday grew bigger she looked for more freedom despite the fact that she had been spayed. She was a very affectionate cat and would follow Joe about like a dog, but just occasionally she would show traces of her tribe and seek to wander alone. Joe was very careful to keep her within range, and during the day when he was at the office, he knew Mrs Massiter would see the cat safely in when she herself was about the hotel.

Mrs Massiter had a small office on the ground floor, but she didn't use it much. She worked closely with Mr Sopwith and liaised with the housekeeper, but mostly she operated on her own, keeping a general eye on the comforts of the guests, satisfying any personal requests, and seeing that any complaint was rectified. She took to her duties with an enthusiasm that surprised even herself and accomplished them with a talent she had been unaware she possessed, and as the weeks went by her complete involvement with the new world washed away the traces of the old. Occasionally she heard from Mr Dawson or Mr Stringer, and there had been a paragraph or two in the Press referring to creditors' meetings and the intentions of the Official Receiver. But she was not directly involved any more, and had put these things out of her mind.

Joe was happy to see how successfully she had adapted herself to their new way of living. The move proved that Sir Vincent Craig had been right; a fully occupied life was the best remedy for the situation in which Mrs Massiter had found herself. The daily—and sometimes evening routine was an effective temporary treatment, and now Joe's only concern was how temporary would it be?

He could visualise long years in London with the prospect of a place in the country receding further away as time went by. For if she was so happy at the Marlborough, why should she go away? How could he suggest it without appearing to put his own self-interest first? But there, perhaps he was looking too far ahead. He was certainly allowing his own pessimism to distort his reasoning. After all, it was early days yet. He supposed it was his own plodding job in the City that brought on these occasional moods of depression. Sometimes, in the narrow confines of his office, when he was sweating over the legends and figures in the thick account books Mr Peebles had passed to him for checking, he would look out of the window and feel that all the freedom of the country was in the little patch of sky he could see between the buildings.

The last letter from Nina had done little to brighten his feelings. She had written from Prague where the Reynaud Company was performing, explaining that it would be some time before they came to London because their present tour appeared to be restricted to Eastern Europe. From Prague they were going to Budapest, and then back to Vienna. Paris had been talked about for the summer, and, of course, she was sure London would follow, but perhaps he could come and see her when the company returned to Vienna?

Joe felt that the chances of his getting to Vienna in the next few months were as remote in the present situation as his moving to the country; but that wasn't the only disturbing note about it all. It was the photograph that Nina enclosed that in some peculiar way seemed to add to his depression. It was a very graceful picture. It showed a supple young man standing tall and holding his arms high and supporting a pretty girl in a typical ballet study. The girl was reaching upward, her arms outspread, one long leg out straight behind her, the other bending at the knee in the form of a V, where her partner held her. It was obviously a skilful manoeuvre, but

Joe wasn't interested in the technicalities; he was more concerned with the caption at the back. *Gustave and me!* Nina had written, and in the letter she had told him with bubbling excitement that they were rehearsing a sequence which they would be dancing together in Budapest.

He didn't know why he should feel so churlish about it. Silly, really. It was only a professional pose. But he would rather had had a picture of Nina alone. Gustave was probably a very nice chap, but the fact that he was there, holding Nina, made Joe feel out of it. They looked a perfect match. So in harmony. But Joe couldn't even get round the floor at a party dance without treading all over his partner's toes. Perhaps that was it. It made him feel—well, inferior. Still, he kept the picture and answered the letter and wished Nina and her partner luck in their new roles.

He had, of course, kept her posted about his own activities. She knew all about the kitten, and their life at the Marlborough, and the job he had in the City; and however exciting her own news she always ended up by asking after Tuesday and Percy as well as Mrs Massiter and himself. So however close her professional partnerships might appear, he should never feel excluded. Yet he did. And the mere fact that Nina had got what she wanted made his own failure more acute.

Through the bright Spring days of April and the long warm days of May, Joe felt the narrow confines of his life even more. While the country breezes carried the scents of the earth after rain, and the air was laden with blossom, his mouth was dry and gritty with the City dust, and he felt like a caged bird in the office in Harrier's Close. His occasional drives into the country with Mrs Massiter on a Sunday only made the Monday routine more irksome, and the summer ahead seemed like an empty promise. He tried to accept his daily environment, to thrust his frustration aside, but how could you, when you were living with it? He never volunteered these feelings to Mrs

Massiter, but sometimes he wondered if she suspected the way he often felt.

It was the letter from Nina at the end of May that jerked his mind away from himself. It was from the Lubitzescu hospital in Budapest, and it was some moments before the shock of the address allowed him to read the contents. She had injured her back. Whilst rehearsing. They had been working very hard and Gustave had suffered a momentary dizziness whilst swinging her high above him in a scene from *Coppelia*. They had both fallen, but she had hit the stage awkwardly, and had hurt her spine. She did not think it serious, but she had to lie flat on her back on a hard bed and it was uncomfortable for her to write, so he must forgive her brief letter and her spidery hand.

Joe could read between the lines how upset she was; not so much from the pain as the thought of missing the opening night of the ballet, and he wrote a long, cheerful letter in reply. Mrs Massiter sympathized, too, and told him to include her thoughts in his letter. She reminded Joe that Nina's energetic training would have kept her very fit, and this would help her make a speedy recovery; but he secretly wondered about that. No matter how fit you were, if the spine was damaged, it might take a very long time.

Joe wrote frequently, often in the quiet of the office after everyone had gone. He always asked Nina if there was anything she wanted, if there was anything he could do, or anything he could send, and she always replied that there was nothing she wished for, except to get better. She had lots of visitors, all from the Company, and that helped her along...

'But you need so much patience,' she wrote. 'I'm not very good at being ill. I'm not in pain any more, but I get so tired lying in this bed when there is so much to do outside. I keep pestering the doctors about getting up, but all they do is nod and smile and tell me to hold on a little longer. I wouldn't mind if the scene changed occasionally, but every day it is the same, and all I can see of the world outside is the summer sky through my window.'

Joe understood. He knew how she felt. And he tried to ease her longing with comforting words. But it wasn't easy to write, to let her see he tried to share her burden. *We seem to have something in common, Nina,* he ended one letter. *We each have a window with a piece of sky in it.*

The days passed and June began to melt away, and Joe felt he should do more than just write letters. If Nina was going to remain in hospital much longer he thought he should go and see her, for once the Reynaud Company had returned to Vienna, she would be entirely alone. He was due for a holiday, but not until the end of August, and that was still too far away. He was sure if he explained the position to Mr Woodfall the dates could be re-arranged. But before he broached the subject, he talked it over with Mrs Massiter.

'I've been thinking about her, too,' Mrs Massiter said. 'Apart from anything else she must feel so lonely in a foreign hospital. Poor Nina, I know that she is very

160

sophisticated and is accustomed to living abroad, but it's different when you're ill.'

'Yes,' said Joe. 'Very different. That's why I feel so badly about not having gone to see her.'

'You can't blame yourself for that, dear. It's a long way to go and it isn't an easy country to get to. But if the treatment is going to take some time, then, of course, you must do something. By all means go and see her, but you can only stay so long, and you can't help much while you're there—I mean, not in any practical way. Wouldn't it be better to try and get her over here?'

'Why—yes. It certainly would. But how?'

She hesitated a moment, and then said slowly, 'Perhaps Vincent could do something.'

'Of course! Sir Vincent Craig.' Joe brought his hands together in an expression of relief. 'Why hadn't I thought of him! He could arrange it, surely?'

'Well, I don't know how much he could do,' she said cautiously. 'But I think you should go and see him.

161

Joe fixed the appointment with Sir Vincent's secretary and worked through his lunch-hour next day so that he could leave the office early. He reached Harley Street soon after four and was shown into Sir Vincent's consulting room on the dot of four-fifteen.

The secretary brought them tea, and during the leisurely interlude, Joe told Sir Vincent about Nina. 'You see, sir,' he ended, 'I've no idea what her injuries are and whether she's getting the best treatment. And if it's going to take a long time, I feel I must do something; but what can I do when she's so far away? We're old friends, and if she was in a hospital here at least I'd feel I was doing something to help by going in and cheering her up.'

Sir Vincent nodded. He was a little amused by the bit about old friends when he knew neither Joe nor the girl were many years old themselves. But he was concerned about her condition, and he thought that for the good of her future alone she should have specialist care.

'I think we can arrange that, Joe,' he

said, putting his cup and saucer gently down on his desk. 'I'll speak to Mr Lancing-Holt. He's orthopaedic, probably the best in the country. We'll get her report from Budapest and then have her flown over.'

Joe suddenly remembered the money.

'That would be splendid, sir,' he said. 'But—er—how about the expense?'

'Don't worry about that now,' Sir Vincent smiled. 'In any event, I should think it certain that your friend is covered by insurance. This Madame Reynaud would have policies for all her dancers designed to take care of accidents of that sort.'

Joe was relieved. 'Yes, of course. I see that now. It's a natural precaution.' He glanced hesitantly at the physician. 'How long would it take, do you think, sir?'

Sir Vincent tapped his fingers thoughtfully on the desk.

'It depends, Joe, on whether she is in a fit condition to travel immediately. If she is, she could be here quite soon. Within the week.' He smiled. 'Do you think that would suit her?'

Joe smiled, too. He'd achieved something at last.

'Yes, sir,' he said. 'That would suit everyone.'

Chapter Ten

On the third Sunday in July when Joe reached the hospital he found Nina out on the verandah. He'd gone into the ward in the usual way, surprised to find her bed empty, and it was the staff nurse who told him where she was.

He went quietly to the glass doors and peered outside wishing to spy her out before she saw him. There were only three patients on the long verandah and Nina was at the end sitting rather stiffly in a collapsible armchair. She was wearing a frilly green dressing-gown and gazing out over the country, the breeze blowing her black hair gently about her shoulders.

Her face still looked a little drawn, but the colour was coming back; nothing like the small, wan face that had smiled up at him from the stretcher when he'd met the plane at London Airport almost a month before. It had been a brief meeting, but she had been grateful for his welcome, and he'd promised to follow her to Marstock next day.

It was a pleasant place to recuperate. The hospital was small and compact and built in a single storey. It stood on the edge of the village, and specialized in the treatment of spinal cases. It was Mr Lancing-Holt's major interest, and although he was available as a consultant in London, he spent most of his time at Marstock. He had certainly taken care of Nina. Her condition had begun to improve from the beginning. She was much happier there (as far as you *could* be happy when you were ill), and that made a difference, too.

Joe was pleased. It was nice to know that you'd been able to help in making someone better although, of course, he realised that little could have been achieved without Sir Vincent Craig. For Joe had never heard of Marstock before; at least, he hadn't known of a hospital there. The grounds were extensive and dotted with shrubs and trees, and the view from the windows across the broad valley was a tireless panorama of soft, relaxing colours. *Get well country!* Mrs Massiter said it was, the first time Joe took her down.

Joe drove down every Sunday and sometimes on Saturday, too. It was only an hour's run from Knightsbridge. On two occasions he had even run down mid-week, leaving the office early, and having a snack in a pub on the way. It made a nice evening and the medical staff never harassed you when it was time to go. Although the clinical routine was there it never seemed apparent. The relaxed, warm atmosphere of the country all around seemed to pervade the hospital. The frequent visits might have appeared a good excuse to take Joe to the country, and indeed, he enjoyed every moment of the journey; but it was only Nina he saw when he was there.

Mrs Massiter had been twice, and once he'd taken Aunt Hilda, Nina's relative from Shepherd's Bush; but not this time. This time he'd brought a rather special visitor, although she was still in the car.

Nina was delighted with the roses, and the chocolates were her favourites, and the guide book of the county would help to pass her time with so many landmarks to identify when she started going for walks.

'Joe!' she exclaimed, bubbling with excitement. 'You shouldn't be so extravagant.' She held the roses close, drawing in their perfume with her breath. 'They're lovely. How did you keep them so fresh?'

'They travelled in a jug of water in the boot,' he said. 'But what about you? You look as fresh as the roses. When did they let you get up?'

'Yesterday. Just for a little while. Today I can stay up the whole afternoon. I wanted to come out here, it's such a lovely day.

'It's a nice surprise seeing you up,' Joe said. 'But I thought the way you looked last time you'd soon be on your feet.'

'I'm still very shaky.' She glanced at the elbow crutches beside her chair. 'They took the plaster jacket off on Wednesday. Then I had more X-Rays. Now I'm wearing a rigid corset. Imagine it! Me in a corset!

But Mr Holt is very pleased with me and says I'll soon be roaming the grounds.' She suddenly put out her hand and her fingers pressed into his arm. Her eyes were large, but the blue was a misty shadow, like a light cloud with tears in it. 'I'm so grateful, Joe, for all you've done. And to all the people here.' She looked away, lowering her eyes so that the long lashes hid them from view. 'I feel a little ashamed.'

'Ashamed?' Joe took the chocolates that would have fallen from her lap as she withdrew her arm. He put them on the table where the roses were. 'What on earth can you be ashamed of?'

'Myself,' she said quietly. 'For thinking about myself when everyone else here thinks only of others.'

'We all think of ourselves, Nina, especially when we are ill. There's nothing to be ashamed of in that.'

'Joe.' She turned her eyes on him again. 'When Mr Holt told me I could get up yesterday, I was so excited. I asked him how soon I could be dancing again. And all he did was smile and say, "We'll see.

You mustn't be impatient, dear. Let's get you walking first."'

'Well, that's good sense. I—'

'But, Joe,' she interrupted him. 'It's what's been worrying me all along, and I'm sure of it now—I'll—never dance again.'

Joe took her hand.

'Now that's not good sense at all,' he said gently. 'Why let your silly imagination spoil everything? Of course you'll dance again. But if Mr Holt had told you so you would have tried to commit him to a date and have gone on worrying the life out of him. He knows what women are,' Joe added, as if he was speaking from experience.

A faint smile curved her mouth then, and he knew the logic of his words was getting through.

'Look,' he said confidentially, 'I've got a surprise for you.'

'Surprise?' Her eyes, clearer now, swept over the contents of the table. 'But you've given me the nicest surprises already.'

'Ah,' he smiled, 'this is rather special.' He got up from the chair, glancing

170

furtively along the verandah. 'Now, if we move you close to the rail.' He carefully eased her chair until it adjoined the wooden balustrade. 'That's it. Now just be patient. I won't be a jiffy.' And leaving her questioning eyes, he hurried along the verandah and down the two steps to the car park. When he came back he was carrying a wicker basket, and any casual observer might have assumed he was out for a picnic; but there was nothing to resemble a picnic inside. He walked right round on the outside of the verandah to the corner where Nina sat.

She was staring at him and the basket.

'What are you doing out there?' she asked.

'Just taking precautions so the nurses don't see,' he said, mysteriously. He unfastened the strap, lifted the lid, and at once a tawny head popped out.

'Oh, Joe!' Nina gasped. 'It's Tuesday! I should have guessed! She's beautiful!'

'I just brought her along to say Hallo,' he said. 'You're always asking what she looks like. I keep meaning to take her photograph—but there, it's much better seeing her in person.'

Nina held her hands over the low rail. 'Give her to me.'

Tuesday stared round and then up at Nina, and slowly rose, placing her white-tipped paws elegantly on the lip of the basket. She remained there for a moment, wondering what all the fuss was about. Then she yawned.

'She's getting heavy,' Joe said. 'Are you sure you ought to hold her?'

'Yes, of course. She hasn't come all this way just to sit out of reach. Let me nurse her.'

'It's the staff I'm afraid of,' Joe said, glancing anxiously along the verandah. 'You're not supposed to bring animals here, I'm sure.' He lifted Tuesday over the rail and placed her gently in Nina's lap. The cat settled down and Nina began to fuss her, murmuring all the while, and it sounded to Joe as if they were both purring.

'How old is she now?' Nina asked.

'Eight or nine months. We never knew her age exactly.'

'Her coat's so downy.' Nina was stroking the long fur. 'How does she get on with Percy?'

'She's never seen him.' Joe smiled. 'He's away this week. We've a relief manager there. Mr Sopwith has taken Percy to the country.' He spoke with his attention elsewhere. He was concerned about the patient along the verandah. The woman was looking at them and smiling.

Nina noticed his expression. 'That's Mrs Wells.'

'She won't say anything?' Joe whispered.

'No. She has two cats of her own. She often talks about them.'

Joe nodded, but was anxious again as he picked up the sound of the tea trolley in the ward.

'You'd better let me have her back, Nina,' he said. 'The tea's coming round, and someone will be out here any minute.'

Reluctantly Nina let Tuesday go as Joe reached over the rail.

'She's really lovely, Joe,' she said. 'No

wonder you're proud of her. She's so affectionate.' Nina watched him settle the cat in the basket and fasten the lid. 'It was a wonderful idea to bring her.'

'I knew you'd like each other,' he said, 'if I could get her in to meet you. I just brought her down on the off-chance, and as soon as I saw you out here I knew the chance had come off. But I'd better take her back to the car now.'

Nina was looking over Joe's shoulder, down the sweep of a broad lawn lined with copper beeches, to the gate in the boundary fence.

'Now, I've a surprise for you,' she said, slyly. 'Look—there. In the meadow.'

He turned round and stared.

A donkey was standing at the gate watching them.

'I saw him there when I came out,' Nina said. 'I wondered if he'd come back when you were here. Go on,' she encouraged in a teasing voice. 'Go down and talk to him.'

The sight of the donkey brought all his memories back, but he couldn't go then.

He had to attend to Tuesday; the tea trolley was coming out. Besides, he was there to be with Nina.

'I'll walk you over next time I come down,' he said. 'And you can introduce me.'

Joe told Mrs Massiter about it that evening when he got back. Not just about the donkey. Everything. But most of all, he talked of Nina's little outburst of depression.

'Poor child,' Mrs Massiter said. 'How sad. Not even her parents to comfort and advise her.'

'She had a letter from her mother in America.' Joe remembered Nina telling him on his last visit. 'She said she hoped to be in England soon. And her father wrote, I think. He's in Spain. But Nina's used to being on her own. I don't think that bothers her now. It's her career she's thinking of. Do *you* think she'll be able to go back to her dancing, Mother?'

'How can I say, dear?' She frowned. 'It's lovely to know she's getting on so well, that she'll be able to lead a normal life; but whether, in time, she could stand up to the strain of her profession, only Mr Lancing-Holt would know. The ballet is so strenuous.'

'It would be nice to be able to encourage her without knowing you're pretending,' Joe said. 'But I don't know Mr Holt. I can't very well ask him. He may not even know himself at the moment.'

'Look, dear, there's plenty of time,' she said soothingly. 'I'm seeing Vincent soon. We're going to have dinner one evening with Mr and Mrs Jefferson. Perhaps there'll be an opportunity for me to find out what Vincent thinks about the girl.'

It was the first Saturday in August that it happened. The day began like any other; it only started to get different later on. Joe was thinking about the afternoon because he was taking Nina out of the hospital for the first time. He was going to take her back, of course, but it was her first real outing and he intended driving her somewhere for tea not too far from Marstock.

He spent most of the morning buying a

pair of shoes. For Nina, of course, or it wouldn't have taken so long. She wanted a nice, easy-fitting pair that were suitable for walking and smart enough for day-time occasions. He had to go to several shops before he could find the style he thought she wanted.

It was almost lunch time when he returned to the hotel, and Tuesday was getting restless. She was accustomed to a longer spell of exercise in the hotel yard on Saturdays and Sundays, and Joe had only given her a few minutes before breakfast. So he took her down to the yard again. He threw her ping-pong ball about but she was more interested in chasing the sparrows and climbing the faded ivy clinging to the wall that hid the yard next door where the dustbins were. So Joe spent most of the time reaching her off the wall and shoo-ing the birds away. When he heard a clock chime one, he knew he couldn't stay any longer, and he swept Tuesday up in his arms and returned to the fourth floor.

He stepped out of the lift and was just passing Mr Sopwith's door when it opened suddenly and a maid hurried out, pulling the door quickly to behind her. She leaned back against it, breathing hard; and Joe knew there was something wrong. In the first place the maid wasn't Lucy, the girl who usually looked after the cleaning of Mr Sopwith's suite as well as the rooms Mrs Massiter and Joe occupied; and the wild look in her eyes suggested that she had just been frightened.

'What's the matter?' Joe asked, pausing in the corridor.

'There's a bird in there.' Her voice was hoarse, choky, as if she'd just swallowed something.

'I know,' Joe said, matter-of-factly.

'A big black bird, it is, sir. Give me a terrible scare, it did. I don't like birds.'

'What were you doing in there, anyway?' Joe asked severely. 'Where's Lucy?'

'Off sick, sir. I'm new here. I only started this week. I'm doing her duties today.' Her eyes rolled over towards the door again. 'It's the bird, sir, that frightens me. It's flying around and talking. Real vicious, it looks.'

'It won't hurt you. Where's Mr Sopwith? It shouldn't be out of its cage.'

'I didn't know it was there. I was using the cleaner—and—this voice spoke and I jumped round—and knocked the cage over. The little door came open—and the bird flew out.' The hushed words spilled over her lips at such a gabbled rate Joe could hardly understand her.

'You mean you let it out!'

'Not on purpose, sir.'

Stupid girl, Joe thought. Mr Sopwith would be in a state. 'I'd better get it,' was all he said.

'Oh—if you could, sir,' she pleaded in anguish now. 'The window's open.'

'Open! Why didn't you say so!' Joe exclaimed, angrily. 'Here—hold on to Tuesday.'

'On to what, sir?' The girl was practically in tears.

'Hold my cat,' Joe said, calming himself down and pushing Tuesday into her arms. 'And don't let her go.'

The girl stood back, and Tuesday immediately began struggling to get out of her rough embrace. Joe stepped forward and opened the door. There was a faint squawk and a sudden flutter of wings and Percy flew out in a curving dive and straight into the lift Joe had just vacated. At the same time Tuesday clawed herself free from the maid's arms, and seeing Percy flash low across the wide corridor, chased after him. Joe rushed in pursuit, but someone below had called the lift, and as he reached the doors they closed silently in his face.

'Now look what's happened!' He felt the rising panic and tried to control it. 'Why didn't you hold on to the cat?'

'I couldn't, sir. It was scratching me.'

'Well, don't stand there. Find Mr Sopwith,' Joe flung at her as he raced down the stairs.

The lift hadn't stopped at the third floor. Nor the second or the first. He didn't know how long it had been at the ground floor when he turned the corner of the staircase and stared at the scene in the reception hall. No one noticed him as he went slowly down the last flight, searching the hall, but there was no sign of Tuesday or the bird. They had obviously been there and left a certain amount of confusion in their wake. A woman was sitting in a chair, her handbag and umbrella on the floor beside it. Her hat was slightly askew, her face looked pasty, and she seemed to be coming out of some kind of faint.

'I couldn't believe it,' Joe heard her telling a tall, bronzed man who appeared to have come to her aid. 'Not in a place like this. I was about to step—h'p—into the lift—h'p—when this huge bird flew—h'p —out on to my hat and—h'p—a cat rushed past my legs—h'p—'

The bronzed man was picking up her handbag and umbrella, the doorman was bringing a glass of water, one of the reception clerks appeared with a bottle of smelling salts, and the other one was on the telephone.

Joe slipped quickly along to the desk.

'Have you seen Mr Sopwith or my mother?' he asked the girl quietly.

'Mr Sopwith's out and I'm trying to call Mrs Massiter,' she said tremulously. 'His bird and your cat came down in the lift.

And they've given that lady hiccups.'

'Which way did they go?' Joe demanded.

'Into the lounge, I think. The hall porter's trying to catch them.'

Joe ran into the lounge, but the porter wasn't there. Neither was the cat or Percy; but a waiter was beckoning to him frantically from the open doors of the restaurant.

'So glad you've come, sir. It's pandemonium in here.' The waiter's words came out in a long sigh of relief as Joe joined him. 'Have you seen Mr Sopwith?'

'I think he's out.'

'Oh, dear. His bird and your cat are in the restaurant, sir.

Joe stood staring into the room. 'Where are they?'

'Over at Mrs Pilkington's table. The head waiter's trying to calm her.'

Joe could see the head waiter and two others now, grouped near a window table. He couldn't see his quarries but he guessed they were up on the curtains somewhere because while the head waiter was attending to the guest the other two men were standing with arms upstretched, like sun-worshippers, apparently trying to coax the truants down. No one else was attempting to do anything. The diners had stopped eating and simply sat back, like a theatre audience, watching the scene by the window.

Joe hurried across. He could see them now. Tuesday clinging to the top of the curtain and Percy perched on the other end of the pelmet, watching her progress.

The waiters made way for Joe as he approached, and he could see they had to hide their smiles. Mrs Pilkington did nothing to hide her disgust.

'Who's this?' she rasped, glaring at Joe. She was a very large woman, festooned in jewellery. She had a loud voice and thick podgy hands and enough diamonds on her fingers to open business in Hatton Garden. A plate of pea soup was still steaming on the table, untouched, and she stood in front of it, the spoon still in her hand, menacing the head waiter.

'This is the young gentleman who owns the cat,' the head waiter explained politely.

'What d'you call it!' she blustered. 'Wild animal, you mean. Leaped across my table. I've never seen anything like it. Is this a hotel or a circus?'

'Not a circus, ma'am. No ring, except those on your fingers. And if you'll pardon my candour, I would suggest you've never seen a wild animal.' The voice, deep and a little lazy, with a faint Western accent, came from just behind Joe, and he turned to find the tall, bronzed man there.

Mrs Pilkington had gasped, but immediately recovered herself.

'Who are you?' she snapped at the stranger. 'The manager?'

'No, ma'am. My name's Halliday and I've just booked in from Canada. I noticed there was a little trouble with the domestic pets, and I thought I could help.'

'Well, I want the manager,' Mrs Pilkington insisted.

'Someone's locating him now,' Halliday said. 'Meanwhile, if you'll just relax we'll attempt to bring the entertainment to an end.' He turned to Joe. 'We'd better get the cat first.'

'Yes, sir,' Joe said. 'She belongs to me.'

Mrs Pilkington was glaring again at the head waiter.

'The nerve of that Canadian!' she breathed.

'Why don't you grow up!' The high-pitched voice of Percy suddenly cut across the momentary silence. And then, in his baritone voice, 'You're a beauty. What time do you go to bed?'

Mrs Pilkington reared up and around, unsure of who had spoken, her face even more livid.

'Insults!' she shrieked. 'I've never been so insulted!'

There was a giggle of laughter from one of the other tables, and this seemed to snap all control.

'I won't stand this a moment longer!' she roared, and smashed the soup spoon down on the table, but it caught the side of the soup plate and the green contents shot into the air, spraying a sticky liquid over herself, the waiters, Halliday and Joe. When she stalked out of the restaurant tears of rage were washing the mascara down her face.

The waiters began clearing up the mess and Joe and Mr Halliday stood grinning at each other as rivulets of soup trickled down their jackets.

'You know,' Halliday said, with a glance up at the pelmet, 'I *thought* that was a Mynah bird.'

It was easier after Mrs Pilkington had gone. And it didn't take long to recapture the runaways. Joe reached Tuesday by standing on the shoulders of Mr Halliday who stood on a chair. Once Tuesday was down and locked in Joe's arms, Percy seemed annoyed the game was over, and he dived down on the cat. Mr Halliday leapt up with open hands and caught the bird in the air. They moved off to the doors together, and everyone resumed eating.

When they entered the lounge they almost bumped into Mrs Massiter hurrying to the restaurant. Her face was flushed and she looked very anxious. She stared at Joe and his companion. They looked so comical with the cat and the bird and soup trickling down their clothes, that she almost forgot her duties.

'This is Mr Halliday, Mother,' Joe said. 'He's just booked in from Canada.'

Mr Halliday was trying to keep a straight face.

'And I've a complaint to make about the soup, ma'am,' he said. 'It's cold.'

Chapter Eleven

People found it easy to take to Brett Halliday. The right kind of people, that is. He was that type of man. Joe took to him from the beginning. And not just because he'd put Mrs Pilkington in her place and had helped Joe out of a nasty situation. He was easy to get on with, had that rugged air of freedom that comes from open spaces, and a patience and understanding for all animals. But what gave the Canadian such an exciting appeal so far as Joe was concerned was that he bred horses, and was looking for a farm in England.

Not that he was really Canadian. He was born in Sussex and had gone to Canada with his parents when he was a boy. Now he was back for a leisurely holiday and looking for a piece of English soil.

'How long are you staying?' Mrs Massiter

asked him when they were sitting in the lounge that evening.

'I've booked here for a month,' he said. 'But I'll probably be extending it. I'm in no hurry. Depends how much success I have.' He was smiling at Mrs Massiter when he spoke, and Joe wondered if he was referring to the purchase of a farm or to anything else.

They were having a late evening drink and Joe had just joined them after returning from Marstock, where he had kept Nina rocking with laughter most of the afternoon recounting his version of the lunch-time scene that day. He hadn't expected to find the new resident entertaining Mrs Massiter when he got back to the hotel; but he was pleased to join them.

It was Mr Halliday's idea. He wanted to make some reparation for driving away their wealthy client, and to thank Mrs Massiter for looking after the cleaning of his suit and attending so promptly to his comforts. He knew it was part of her job; but he wanted to show his appreciation just the same, and had suggested an evening drink.

Halliday talked freely about his ranch in Canada and hinted at some of his future plans, and Joe realised that here was someone who'd made an unqualified success of living the life he wanted. Although he was more than double Joe's years, he created that feeling between them that put them on equal terms. Joe supposed it had something to do with their mutual respect for animals. It was an instant recognition of a common bond between them. Even Mr Sopwith noticed, and warmed to him. And he only stopped by for a moment to thank their guest for all he had done during the unfortunate scene that day.

Joe spoke of it to Mrs Massiter when they were back in their suite that night, after he'd told her how well Nina was progressing.

'You know, Mother,' he said, thoughtfully, 'I think we ought to make a friend of Mr Halliday. He's on his own and he doesn't seem to know anyone over here.'

'I think you *have* made a friend of him,' she smiled.

'No, what I mean is—I think we should help him.'

'Help him? I think Mr Halliday is the kind of man who gets by very well on his own.'

'You can always do with some friendly advice when you're a stranger in a country,' Joe said, with a wise look.

'Now what advice do you think *we* should give him, Joe?'

'Well, about finding a farm, for instance.'

'I don't think we could advise a man like Mr Halliday on his own business, dear. Not unless he asked.'

But in the days that followed that is what Brett Halliday appeared to do. Ask. Not directly, but in all kinds of devious ways. He discussed the price of land, and sought their opinions on the most favourable areas, and showed them particulars and photographs of properties agents had on their books. He went to see several places, and once suggested to Mrs Massiter that when he found a likely farm perhaps she would go along and give her opinion. But his queries weren't limited to business. He asked Mrs Massiter's advice on places to see in London; the best restaurants, the worthwhile plays; and once he'd turned up with two theatre tickets and asked her to go along.

Joe told Nina about it when he went down to Marstock.

'He sounds very nice,' Nina said. 'I'm looking forward to meeting him.'

They were sitting under the oak beams in the Cosy Cot Tea Shoppe in Wickham Pump, a village twelve miles from Marstock. They often went there to tea when Joe came down and took her away from the hospital on Saturday and Sunday afternoons.

'He wants to meet you,' Joe said. 'He knows your history now.'

'You shouldn't talk about your friends,' she teased, and then, looking serious, she asked, 'Is he married?'

'No, I don't think so. Why?'

'Seems to me he likes your mother.'

'I don't know about that. He's friendly

with everyone. But he's really keen on horses.'

Nina smiled.

'You can't live with horses all the time,' she said. After a moment her expression changed again, excited with a new thought. She leaned forward, speaking softly although no one was there to hear. 'Joe, supposing Mr Halliday does get a farm. Do you think he'd give you a job on it?'

'Well, of course, nothing's been said about that. But he knows about my past, and what I've learned in the country. You know, when I was a boy. I told him about Smokey and the fun we had at Valley End. And he knows my real ambition; how much I'd like to work with animals. He seemed really interested. But I don't know what would happen if he bought a place. I suppose he'd have a manager to run it, at least, till he came over here to live. And I think I could be useful. To start with I could do the farm accounts, couldn't I?' he ended with a grin.

'It would be wonderful, Joe, if it

happened like that. I do hope it will.' She was silent again, and then she flashed her eyes at him in another teasing look. 'Now, I've got some wonderful news about myself,' she said. 'I'm leaving hospital for good next week.'

'Nina!' Joe exclaimed, reaching across the table to squeeze her hand and nearly knocking over the teapot. 'That's marvellous. Why didn't you tell me the news at once?'

'I wanted to save it up and have it with the cream cakes,' she said.

Nina was leaving the hospital on the Saturday, but she had to return in a fortnight to see Mr Lancing-Holt, and although she was going to stay with Aunt Hilda at Shepherds Bush it was arranged she should spend the first weekend with Joe and Mrs Massiter. Joe was going to collect her Saturday morning and as that began his fortnight's holiday, he planned to take Nina out to the country and the coast each day.

It was about the middle of that week, before Joe's holiday began, that Mrs

Massiter told him the news.

'It looks as if Brett's found the place he wants at last,' she said.

'He has? Where?'

'West Sussex. Near Wyeford.'

'Wyeford?' Joe was seeing an imaginary map of the county. 'Where's that?'

'About ten miles north of Chichester. Local agents are dealing with it and Brett's still down there. I don't know when he's coming back, but he wants us to go down and see it on Saturday.'

Joe looked disappointed. 'Saturday? That's the day I'm collecting Nina from the hospital,' he said.

Mrs Massiter didn't look disappointed at all. She was smiling.

'I know,' she said. 'I told Brett that and he said why not bring her, too?'

'What a splendid idea.' Joe began to work out a time-table without delay. 'Let's see, now. We'd better meet you down there. Say at twelve o'clock. I'll send Nina a card and tell her I'm coming early because we're going on to Chichester.' He chuckled. 'That'll give her something to think about,' he said.

Saturday was a lovely day. Just the day to come out of hospital or start your holiday or see a farm. The sun was hot and the breeze no more than a cool whisper, so Joe had the hood down. Nina settled comfortably in the passenger seat, her back supported with a cushion.

'What is this mystery about Chichester you wrote on your card?' she asked.

'Be patient,' Joe smiled, stowing her luggage in the boot. 'Let's get moving first.'

He drove out of the hospital grounds and on to the road before satisfying her curiosity.

'It's a farm,' he said. 'Whitegates. Just outside the village of Wyeford.'

'You mean—Mr Halliday's bought it?' Nina's voice bubbled with excitement.

'Well, no, not yet. But it looks as if he will. He came back last night and said it was just what he wanted. And Mother's gone down with him this morning. He wants her opinion. And mine, too. He's

196

a rare one for opinions,' he added with a smile.

'Joe, how wonderful. And how kind to invite me along.'

'He'll probably be glad of your opinion, too,' he teased. 'We're meeting them there at twelve.'

'What sort of farm is it?'

'Don't know, exactly. But there are horses there.' Joe frowned. 'It seems there's a main farmhouse; the manager's in that. Lays back off the road down a long drive. But Whitegates is another house, further along. It's all part of the farm. That's where we have to meet.'

'Well, let's get on,' Nina urged. 'I can't wait to see the place.'

Joe drove faster, but not too fast for comfort. He was careful not to give Nina a bumpy ride. But she seemed unconscious of anything but the intoxicating delight of being free once more. She sat with her head up, her face slightly tilted towards the sky, the breeze stealing tendrils of her hair and throwing them behind like woodsmoke in the wind. He stole a glance at her from time to time, wondering about her future.

'What did Mr Lancing-Holt have to say?' he asked at length.

'That I'm a credit to him.' She lazily turned her head and smiled. 'He says I've got to go carefully for a while. Nothing strenuous—you know,' she said, and the smile faded a little. 'He's going to keep tabs on me. I have to see him again in a fortnight.'

'Did he say anything about dancing? In time, I mean.'

'No. Neither did I.'

'Well, I've been making soundings for you. I got Mother to ask Sir Vincent Craig. It took her a little while but she spoke to him on the 'phone the other evening.'

Nina was looking ahead through the windscreen now. She did not turn or say anything.

'He's a friend of Mr Holt's,' Joe went on gently. 'And the verdict is that there's no reason why you shouldn't go back to ballet given time.'

He expected her to turn and smile and

gurgle with joy; but she continued to look ahead.

'I don't know that I want to now,' she said. She spoke without any trace of bitterness or rancour; more with relief. She turned then, appealing to him. 'Oh, Joe, I don't know what I am going to do—or even what I want to do. I've been in a different world—and away from the one I knew for so long. Madame Reynaud wants me back. Mother is coming to see me. She wants me to return with her to America. I'm just confused.'

'It'll sort itself out,' he said.

'But haven't you ever felt like that, Joe? All muddled up?'

Joe nodded.

'Yes,' he said. 'I've felt like that.'

It wasn't easy to find Whitegates. Twice Joe drove through the village and out the other side looking for the lane that led to the farm. In the end, he stopped and asked a local.

'Whitegates,' the old man repeated slowly. 'Ay, you'll be almost there. Jes' take thar second turnin' on ye left—Tyler's

Lane they calls it—an' ye'll find the house on the right past the 'orses 'ome.'

Joe looked at him hard. 'What home?'

'The 'orses 'ome. Ye'll be seein' it, lays back it do, on ye right.'

Joe thanked him and let in the clutch.

'Wonder what he means—calling it a horses' home?' Nina said.

'Probably some local tag because there's some old horses there.' Joe turned into the lane. On either side, undulating hedges screened their view of the fields, but here and there they could see the harvest going on, though mostly it was pasture land.

After a mile the fields and meadows on the right gave way to a copse and beyond were smart white posts and wire fencing set back from the verge. They saw the farmhouse at the end of the drive, and a five bar gate closing the entrance. There was a board near the gate and in the meadows around the house and buildings, horses grazed.

'We go on a little further,' Joe said, as he drove slowly past. 'Whitegates is the next house.'

'But didn't you see what was on the board by the gate, Joe?' Nina was looking at him in some surprise. 'I didn't get the name, but it said *Home for Retired Horses.*'

'Well,' Joe said, 'it must be all part of the farm. We'll find out for sure in a moment.'

There was another copse of firs and birches to their right and just beyond a neat hedge with a house behind it. The gates were open and Joe swung into the short drive.

It was a nice place. Not a cottage or a farmhouse. Something between the two. But the Jaguar Brett Halliday had hired for his stay was nowhere to be seen.

'What a beautiful old house,' Nina said as Joe helped her out of the car. 'I wonder how long it's been empty?'

Joe was looking around as if he'd lost something. 'Mother and Brett should be here, but where's the car?'

Nina walked slowly to the timbered porch. 'Perhaps they've gone round to see the farm manager.' She stepped close to the oak door, noticing a square of paper held in place by the heavy knocker. Curious, she pulled it free, and saw the writing on it.

'Look, Joe,' she said. 'Someone's left a note.' She handed it to him, and he smiled.

'It's from Mother,' he said, reading quickly. 'They've gone back to Chichester to see the agent before the office closes. They've left the door unlocked and the key inside. We're to look round, and meet them for lunch at the Landsdowne Hotel.' He opened the door. 'She says be sure and lock up when we leave and take the key.'

It was a large hall with a curving white-painted staircase. The boarded floor was of dark oak, and panelled doors opened off on either side of them. The key lay on the low sill of the hall window. Joe put it in his pocket, and looked at Nina.

'Where shall we start?' he said.

'In here first.' She opened the door on their right.

It didn't take long to size up the two front rooms and the kitchen, the well-fitted cupboards and the shelf-lined store room. It was in the large room at the back where they paused the longest.

It was a nice room, painted white with a beamed ceiling and a red-brick fireplace. But the nicest thing of all was the window. Tall and wide, it was. A picture window of country and sky. Looking through it you could follow the gentle slope of the garden path to a kissing-gate in the boundary hedge, and beyond it a meadow with willow trees on the further side and a lazy stream sparkling in the sun. The garden was rough and overgrown, but the roses were alive and there were apples on the trees, and the scent of honeysuckle seeped into the room.

'How lucky for someone to have a view like this,' Nina said, dreamily. 'Do you really think Mr Halliday will buy?'

'I don't know if he's made up his mind,' Joe said, 'but I expect he'll decide today.'

Nina turned, looking at him. 'But just suppose he does, Joe. How would it work out—for you and your mother, I mean?'

'Well, how can I say what his plans

would be—but the farmhouse has the manager in, and Brett's got to go back to Canada. When he returns he's sure to run the farm himself and where would he live but in the farmhouse?' Joe paused, a hopeful smile curving his mouth. 'And if he gave me a job...'

'You mean, then,' Nina said, softly, 'you might live here?'

He stepped closer, his eyes holding hers.

'*We* might live here, Nina,' he said. 'If you don't go away for too long.'

He was very close now. Only one step more; but before he took it his eye was attracted to the window. And suddenly he was staring down the garden path.

'Look, Nina. Down by the gate!' He turned her gently round, his arm circling her shoulders.

'A donkey!' she said.

'And another!' They both stood staring through the picture window.

'Where have they come from?' Nina wondered.

'They must be on the farm,' Joe said.

Nina squeezed Joe's hand.

'Isn't that another one—over there?' She pointed towards a gap in the hedge.

'Where?' Joe moved slightly to get a better view. 'Why—so there is.' He couldn't believe his eyes. Three donkeys—all coming to the gate.

'And—look—' whispered Nina. 'There's another...'

And so there was. And another... And another... And another...

This Large Print Book for the Partially sighted, who cannot read normal print, is published under the auspices of

THE ULVERSCROFT FOUNDATION